Tighe grinned at her from under the brim of his cowboy hat.

"It's awesome that you're pregnant with triplets, babe."

"It is not awesome. I mean, it is, but you're not, so don't tweak me."

He laughed. "In a week or two, you'll be trying to drag me to the altar."

"I don't think so."

His navy eyes practically danced with pride. He was really impressed with himself. River sighed and looked away.

"I'm so amazed by you," Tighe said.

She turned to face him. "Why?"

"Because you're such a fertile goddess. I would never have suspected you'd be the Callahan woman to turn up a three-in-a-row."

He grinned, the handsomest man she'd ever seen, and River wanted to smack him ever so badly.

Dear Reader,

In this fourth book of the Callahan Cowboys miniseries, Tighe Callahan sets out to prove he's a better man than his twin, Dante, and does so by attempting to ride Firefreak, a rank bounty bull. This is the beginning of Tighe's path of discovery, which ultimately leads him to the strong and capable River Martin.

I invite you to join this tough and adventurous family as they strive to keep Rancho Diablo, the home of their hearts, safe from those who wish them ill, while trying to tame their own wild spirits. Is there anything more fun than watching two people struggle against their destiny as they fall in love? You know that at Rancho Diablo, there's always a happy ending—and a magic wedding dress to seal the deal!

Best wishes always,

Tina

CALLAHAN COWBOY
TRIPLETS

—

TINA LEONARD

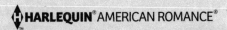
HARLEQUIN® AMERICAN ROMANCE®

Recycling programs
for this product may
not exist in your area.

ISBN-13: 978-0-373-75469-4

CALLAHAN COWBOY TRIPLETS

Copyright © 2013 by Tina Leonard

Printed in U.S.A.

ABOUT THE AUTHOR

Tina Leonard is a *USA TODAY* bestselling and award-winning author of more than fifty projects, including several popular miniseries for Harlequin American Romance. Known for bad-boy heroes and smart, adventurous heroines, her books have made the *USA TODAY,* Waldenbooks, Ingram and Nielsen BookScan bestseller lists. Born on a military base, Tina lived in many states before eventually marrying the boy who did her crayon printing for her in the first grade. You can visit her at www.tinaleonard.com, and follow her on Facebook and Twitter.

Books by Tina Leonard

HARLEQUIN AMERICAN ROMANCE

My heartfelt gratitude to all the loyal and supportive readers who believe in a Callahan way of life.

Chapter One

*"You can drive yourself crazy trying to outfox
a Callahan. That goes double for the Callahan
women."*
—Bode Jenkins, neighboring ranch owner bragging
a bit about his three Callahan granddaughters to a
reporter

Tighe Callahan sized up the enormous spotted bull
that eyed him warily. "Hello, Firefreak," he said. "You
may have bested my twin, Dante, but I aim to ride you
until you're soft as glove leather. Gonna retire you to
the kiddie rides."

The legendary badass rank bull snorted a heavy
breath his way, daring him. Dark eyes glared attitude
and a *no-you-won't* warning.

"You're crazy, Tighe," his brother Jace said. "I'm
telling you, that one wants to kill you."

"Feeling's mutual." Tighe grinned and knocked on
the wall of the pen. "If Dante stayed on him for five
seconds, I ought to at least go ten."

Jace looked at Tighe doubtfully. "Sure. You can do
it. Whatever." He glanced around. "I think I'll go get
some popcorn and find a pretty girl to share it with.

You and Firefreak just go ahead and chat about life. May be a one-sided conversation, but those are your favorite, anyway."

Jace wandered off. Tighe studied the bull, which never broke eye contact with him, his gaze wise from the scores of cowboys he'd mercilessly tossed, earning himself a legendary status.

"I'm a real believer in the power of positive thinking, old son," Tighe told his horned adversary. "And I'm positive that tomorrow my name will live on as the first cowboy to ever pin a bull's-eye on you and hit it dead center. See, I figure it was destiny that I finally drew you. And what you don't know is that I've got a secret training regimen. You think you're tough, but you don't know tough until you've spent a couple years being ridden by Callahan tots. You only have to do your job for eight seconds, throw off a cowboy or two. Me? My job can go on for hours. I'm tough as nails, my spotted nemesis."

Firefreak's response was to throw a hoof his way, crashing into the wall of the pen, which thundered under the blow. Tighe tipped his hat and turned to go.

"Hi, Tighe," a feisty little darling he knew too well said, and Tighe stopped dead in his tracks.

"Sawyer Cash, what are you doing here?" He glanced around. If Jace had seen Sawyer—the new nanny bodyguard at Rancho Diablo and daughter of Storm Cash, their neighbor and a man they weren't too sure they trusted—he would have run up the red flag of danger. Jace had never mentioned it, but Tighe was pretty sure his brother had a thing for the petite redhead.

"Hi, Tighe," River Martin said, coming to join Sawyer, and Tighe felt his heart start to palpitate. Now here

was his dream, his unattainable brunette princess—
even though he liked to tell his family he secretly had
River in the bag—smiling at him, as sweet as cherry
wine. "We heard you're going to ride a bull tomorrow,
so the girls and I decided to come out and watch. Your
sister, Ash, is here, too, but she's chatting up some
cowboys. Said she wasn't interested in watching you
meet your doom."

This wasn't a good sign. A man didn't need his con-
centration wrecked by a gorgeous female—and right
now, Tighe had a twist in his gut even a few beers
wouldn't chase off. Nor did he want said gorgeous,
unattainable female to see him get squashed by a few
tons of angry luggage with horns. A man needed to
seek his holy grail and stare death in the eyes in order
to realize that he was but a speck on this earth, and if
the woman he adored didn't reciprocate his feelings,
well, there were worse things. Like getting stomped
into dust by a rank bull.

Dante'd had his five seconds on Firefreak without
the woman he loved witnessing his ultimate crash into
reality.

But River was smiling at him with her teasing eyes
that sent him over the moon, so all Tighe could say
was, "Nice of you ladies to come out." *To witness my
humiliation. I was riding on guts and bravado, and
somehow that particular cocktail of courage has suddenly left me stone-cold.*

River said, "Good luck," and Tighe shivered, because he did believe in magic and luck and everything
spiritual. And any superstitious man knew it was taunt-
ing the devil himself to wish a cowboy good luck when
the challenge he faced in the ring was nothing com-

pared to the real challenge: forcing himself to look into
a woman's sexy eyes and not drown.

He was drowning, and he had been for oh, so long.

TEN MINUTES LATER, Tighe was sitting in his truck and
considering spending the night there. He'd had an offer
to bunk in with some rodeo buddies, but he was in the
mood to be alone.

Actually, he was in the mood to hunt up River, but
pride wouldn't allow him to chase that little goddess
down. He was woefully aware he'd gotten something
of a reputation among his six siblings for being a love-
starved schmuck, which was odd because he'd previ-
ously held a pretty impressive record for being catnip
to the ladies. Galen, the eldest, was a medical doctor,
but really enjoyed touting his skills as a diviner of the
heart, never more than when he was ribbing Tighe
about the state of his brunette heartburn. His twin,
Dante, left him pretty much alone because he knew he
he'd been darn lucky to catch River's best friend and
fellow nanny bodyguard, Ana St. John. Jace thought
he knew things but didn't—though that didn't stop him
from snickering at Tighe's unrequited longing. Sloan,
married to Kendall and the proud father of adorable
twin sons, cut him some slack because he knew how
much it stank when a man couldn't seem to reel in the
woman of his every waking thought. Falcon was happily married now and enjoying life with his baby girl,
so he considered himself fortunate and offered no decent advice. Their sister, Ashlyn, was full of witty ri-
postes about Tighe's lackluster attempts to woo River,
but she'd been chasing the prince of her pining, Xav
Phillips, for a couple of years now, with all the luck of
a sleep-struck princess.

"I'm on my own," Tighe muttered, and then a voice said, "Hi, Tighe," and he about jumped out of his boots.

"Hi, River," he said, his throat suddenly thick like a tree trunk and about as useful for talking. "Where's Sawyer?"

She glanced over her shoulder. "Torturing Jace."

"It's good for him. Pretty sure she's up to the job." He wished he could kiss her, but how would she react? "I need to head off and find a motel. Did you need something?"

She shrugged, and the gesture made her breasts move under her blue, short-sleeved dress. "You can stay with me," River said, and he had to tighten his jaw so it didn't crash to the parking lot.

"Stay with you?" he repeated.

"Mmm-hmm." She smiled at him, and it was all he could do not to shout, *hell yes!* and jump into the canyon of lost sense. "I've got my own room at Sherby's," River said.

Sherby's was a quaint B and B outside Santa Fe. He knew Sherby and his wife, Anne—they were great rodeo fans and had done a fair bit of horse trading in their day. Good, honest folk. "I'm not sure Anne would care for me lodging with you, River."

"We won't tell her I've got double occupancy." She winked at him, cute as a doe, and Tighe's blood began a pounding unlike anything he could ever remember feeling—not even when he was in Afghanistan with Dante and they were trying to keep from picking grit out of their teeth and bullets out of their appendages. He had the scar from one he hadn't managed to avoid, which had lodged itself in his biceps, right under the lightning strike tattoo all the Chacon Callahan siblings wore: the sign of their bond.

"I'm not sure where there may be a vacancy," Tighe murmured doubtfully, trying to hang on to whatever fragments of good sense he possessed.

"And you probably won't find one now. Everything is full."

Dante and he had never worried much about where they were going to stay. One or the other of them always made a reservation, or they slept in their trucks. Might have been an awkward lifestyle with anyone else, but he and Dante had been each other's shadow all their lives, and especially on the rodeo circuit. No one knew Tighe like Dante did.

In fact, it had been a little lonely since Dante had gotten married. Not that he wasn't extremely happy for his knuckleheaded twin—but Tighe did miss his shadow on occasion.

"Come on," River said, "get your stuff. I promise not to lay a hand on you, big guy." She turned and walked off, leading the way, hips swaying, the lure of the wild loudly calling to Tighe, and all he could think was *Rats. Kinda wish she wasn't so good at keeping promises.*

Riding Firefreak for the full eight seconds was more likely than him catching that hot angel.

He grabbed his duffel and followed.

RIVER SNEAKED TIGHE in under cover of night, through a back door so none of the other guests—nor Anne Sherby—would notice she was keeping company. For one thing, everyone staying at Sherby's was female, and River wasn't sharing. For another, what good was it to have a secret crush if the whole world figured it out?

Catching a Callahan wasn't easy, and tonight, she intended to catch this one in a snare that might interest him. She had a deck of cards and a bottle of something Ashlyn said the Callahan guys liked to sip on in their upstairs library meetings at Rancho Diablo—and a comfy bed. Oh, she had absolutely no plans to seduce this cowboy—that would be dirty pool—but it wouldn't hurt a bit if they spent a little time together away from the Callahan clan of prying eyeballs and matchmaking roulette. Just to see what would happen…

"Put your duffel there," she said, pointing to a spot under the window in the tiny room.

"Whoa," Tighe said, observing the twin bed in Miss Sherby's B and B. "Do you think maybe Ms. Anne's got a futon or a sleeping bag we could discreetly inquire about?"

River smiled. "We'll manage."

"I've seen baby cribs bigger than that bed."

"Dante says you guys have shared a truck many times. This bed is about the size of a cab, isn't it?"

"Yeah, but he's my twin."

She smiled and pulled out the deck of cards and the whiskey bottle. "I don't drink, but Ash says this is your favorite."

"Wait a minute, little lady," Tighe said. "What's going on here? I've known you for about two years, and we've rarely been in the same room, much less a bed. And you brought my drink of choice. Are you setting me up?"

Of course she was setting him up. She wasn't certain it was the best idea, but she'd been asked to play this role by the Callahans. *So here I am.*

"You mean am I seducing you?" River considered him. "Do you want me to?"

His handsome face was puzzled, maybe even perplexed. He was such a gentleman—all the Callahans were—and all that chivalry kept him from wanting to make a mistake of the sexual variety.

"Don't worry," River said. "If you're that concerned about it, I'll flip you for the bed. Or beat you at twenty-one for it."

He grinned. "You can't beat me, lady. I was born playing cards, pool and hooky."

She poured him a drink. "You're going to need a shot of this for courage."

"For Firefreak? I don't need anything to give me courage for that oversize piece of shoe leather." Still, he gulped down the whiskey.

"It's getting late," River said.

"True. I'll let you have the bed, gorgeous, and I'll take the floor. Use my duffel as my pillow."

"All right. I'm going to change." She slipped into the bathroom, took off her dress, put on a pair of sleep shorts and a T-shirt. Very modest, but still feminine. Why had she allowed the Callahans to talk her into this caper? Sawyer claimed that the only way to a man's heart was making him see you, really notice you. So that you were unforgettable to him.

River was pretty certain she'd been forgettable to Tighe for the two years she'd been guarding Sloan and Kendall's twins. Taking a deep breath, she thought about those dark navy eyes, the longish, almost black hair that begged her to run her fingers through it, the hard, strong muscles…and then she opened the door to do her job.

"Hey," Jace said, and River nearly shrieked.

"He found me," Tighe said. "He's like a homing pigeon. An ugly one, but just the same, a pigeon."

"Hi, Jace," she said, not surprised at all to see him.

The plan was proceeding as outlined, even if she didn't feel all that good about the plot on Tighe.

"He's got no place to stay, either. Mind if he bunks with us?" Tighe asked.

"I promise not to snore." Jace poured himself a drink. "Ms. Sherby sure knows how to stock the stuff a guy likes."

"Fine by me." River wished Jace hadn't shown up so soon. Secretly she'd been hoping for just a couple moments alone with her dream cowboy. She sat on the bed, waited for Jace's signal.

"You're the luckiest woman in town, spending the night with two Callahans," he said as he dumped his duffel on the floor, not sounding anything like a man who was out to derail his brother.

"Good times, good times," River said, but her in-sincerity was lost on the two men as they shuffled the deck, splayed the cards on the small table and began a spirited game.

"You're just determined to ride that piece of ugly spotted steak tomorrow, aren't you?" Jace asked.

"You better believe it. I'm going to ride him like a little girl's pony."

River rolled her eyes. "Sexist, much?"

"Not at all. But we give gentle rides to the ladies," Jace said. "You wouldn't want to give a woman a mount that might harm her in any way."

River rolled her eyes at the typical Callahan non-sense she'd heard many times. "Jace, why aren't you riding tomorrow?"

"Thought about it. Decided I'm too good-looking to risk injuring myself on a bull." He laughed. "My brother here is on his own personal mission to separate his brain from his skull."

"Why?" River looked at Tighe, and he glanced at her, his gaze catching on her lips, it seemed, and then lower. It was the first time she could ever remember him looking at her for more than a second. She decided to see if she could get his attention off his cards, let him slowly figure out what he was missing out on. "What do you have to prove?"

"Nothing." Tighe tossed his cards onto the table, grinned at Jace. "You lose. Deal."

Clearly, he wasn't going to take the bait. Jace poured his brother another shot. Tighe slurped it down, sighing with happiness. "This is fun. I'm finally starting to relax." He glanced at her, his gaze hitting about chest level. "Anybody else think it's hot in here?"

Jace glanced at River, surreptitiously winked. She shrugged, then got up and raised the window, which would only serve to heat the room a little more. "Maybe the breeze will help."

Tighe seemed to find her legs quite interesting as she sat cross-legged on the bed.

"I win," Jace said. "What do you know? I finally beat you." He scooped the cards up, but Tighe didn't take his gaze away from River.

"Let's see what's in this goody basket." She rose, checked out the treats Ms. Sherby put in every room.

"I'm getting tired," Tighe said. "Think I'll call it a night. My ride's at ten, and I want to be ready to rock." He got down on the floor, shoved his duffel under his head. "This is great. Thanks, River, for letting us stay."

"Have another toddy," Jace said. "It'll help you sleep." He handed his brother another shot, which Tighe quickly downed.

"If I didn't know better, I'd think you kids were trying to get me tipsy. Won't work, you know. I've got a hollow leg."

"Excuse me," River said, "did you say you have a hollow head?"

"Ha. You sound like one of my brothers now. Actually, like my sister, Ash."

Tighe didn't say anything else, and a moment later, sonorous snoring rose from the floor.

"That's it," Jace said, "he's out like a light. Never could hold his liquor."

"Now what?" River stared at the example of her perfidy sleeping like a baby at the foot of her bed. "Seems so mean to try to keep him from riding. He says it's his holy grail. Aren't Callahans fairly wedded to their holy grails? Seems like bad juju to try to keep one from his goal."

"Trust me, Tighe can't ride worth a flip. He's really only suited for the kiddie calf catch." Jace shrugged, then grinned the famous Callahan grin. "Now you just head off to your room, and I'll take care of Brother Bonehead."

Certainly, no one could say the Callahans weren't a different breed. A job was a job, and this caper had been part of hers. Even the beloved aunt of the Callahan clan, Fiona, had been in on this gig, sanctioning Jace to do whatever he could to keep Tighe off Firefreak. "If you're sure. I'm next door, if you need anything."

"One thing about you, River, we know we can always count on you to do whatever has to be done."

She wasn't sure she felt good about that compliment at the moment. With another glance at the handsome hunk on the floor, River grabbed her stuff and headed to her own room.

It might be the only time she ever had Tighe in a

bedroom, and oh, how she hoped it wasn't. But once he figured out her part in this escapade, there was no way he'd see her as anything but the woman who'd destroyed his dream, smashed his holy grail to pieces.

Which was no way to catch the man you'd been fantasizing about for the longest time.

She went into her room and closed the door. Got into bed, stared at the ceiling. As a bodyguard, she stuck to her assignment. Watching over the twins, Carlos and Isaiah, was her pride and joy.

Tonight had been a mission, no reason for regret. Tomorrow, she'd be back with Sloan and Kendall's little boys, and that was all that mattered.

Wasn't it? Not that sleeping cowboy she was helping to divert from his dream?

He was never going to forgive her for her role in his distraction.

RIVER HAD NEARLY fallen asleep, was drifting on a cloud of guilt and soft-focus sexy fantasies of Tighe, when she heard the door quietly open. She sat up, peering through the darkness. "Sawyer?"

"Not exactly, gorgeous," Tighe said, sliding into bed, pulling her up against his rock-hard body. "You shouldn't let Jace talk you into things, babe, he's a newb." Tighe kissed her neck, and hot, dizzying tingles shot all over her. "But since you're just so darn sweet—and because I know Jace dragged you into his dumb scheme—I'm going to give you another chance to try to keep me off that bull."

Chapter Two

The next afternoon, River sat in the bleachers at the rodeo, waiting for Tighe to get himself squished. Jace seemed certain his brother couldn't ride very well. River had no reason to doubt Jace and Ash's reasoning for trying to stop Tighe, or their aunt Fiona's, for that matter, although Fiona's motives could be suspect at times.

After Tighe made love to her last night, he'd kissed her, told her she was darling and cute as a button, and that he'd think about her every second today, except when he was on the back of Firefreak.

Tighe was, in a word, an ass.

Jace slid onto the bleacher next to her, handing her some popcorn.

"Hey," he said. "Fancy meeting you here."

"Yeah. You, too." She overlooked the corny greeting, her gaze searching for Tighe among the cowboys in the arena.

"Funny thing. I lost sight of my brother last night."

"Did you?" River didn't dare glance his way. The Callahans might have hatched a plot to keep Tighe off his nemesis, but she'd been completely unable to resist his charming persuasion.

"I did. Tighe was nowhere to be found." Jace shook his head. "I think I might have sipped a little too liberally from Tighe's libation. My head's killing me." He handed her a soda off a cardboard tray he'd carried into the bleachers. "You didn't see him?"

She shook her head. It wasn't a total fib—she *hadn't* seen Tighe in the darkness. But she'd felt him, and he'd made glorious love to her that she'd remember for days.

"Don't know where he went. I looked for him near the pens, but no one's seen him." Jace shrugged. "He hasn't scratched, either, which is a bad sign that our plan didn't work."

"*Your* plan," River said. "I refuse to take further part in keeping Tighe from his…goal."

Jace glanced at her. "I don't blame you. He's a rascal."

"You're all rascals. Including your sister, Ashlyn, and your aunt Fiona."

Jace laughed. "No argument there. But we're doing what's best for him. Ever since Tighe was little, he thought he was a big shot."

"How is he different from, say, you?"

"Because I can do what I brag about. Tighe isn't Dante. He isn't smart like Galen. He's not tough like Ash. If it's true what Grandfather Running Bear says about one of us being the hunted one, the one who'll bring destruction to the family, it'd be Tighe. He's always on a quest, but he never quite achieves it. You get what I'm saying?"

"I don't want to talk about it," River said, "I've worked for the Callahans for quite a while. I know the drill."

"I wouldn't have thought you'd feel guilty, River. Your job is to be a bodyguard. Protecting Callahans is what you do, right?" Jace leaned back, a popcorn-eating philosopher. "Protecting Tighe from himself is no different from your normal job description."

"Whatever." River's nerves were jangling. "I don't feel guilty, just for the record."

"You did the best you could."

"Shush, Jace," she said, "I can't hear the announcer. I don't want to miss Tighe ride."

"True, if we blink we'll miss him," Jace said, laughing.

"You guys are mean. Tighe's on a mission." River felt compelled to stand up for him, even if she'd been part of the plot to keep him off the bounty bull. Secretly, she hoped Tighe met his desired goal, whatever it was that urged him on—because then...

Then he might want to settle down like his Callahan brothers, Sloan, Falcon and Dante.

That was treacherous thinking. One night of sexy lovemaking didn't mean anything—at least, it probably hadn't to Tighe.

But it had to her. If the opportunity presented itself again, she doubted she'd refuse another night in Tighe's arms.

In fact, she knew she wouldn't.

She might even instigate it.

IT WAS TIME: the moment of truth. Either he could take it or he couldn't; it was time to find out if he could pin the tail on the donkey.

"Good luck," said Galen, who'd come out to watch his fall from grace. But Tighe had told him in no uncertain terms that he was going to stay on Firefreak for the whole eight seconds, come hell or high water.

"Thanks." He took a deep breath, approached the chute. "Is River watching?"

"I'm sure she has every intention of watching you win the buckle, bro," Galen said, and Tighe swallowed hard.

"Great." He had to make eight seconds. What price being a hero? Priceless, no matter how many bruised ribs. He got on the chute amid muttered encouragement from the other cowboys helping load up Firefreak's slayer. He mounted the massive body, which had been relatively still until he seated himself, and began wrapping his hand—then crashes, curses and fear rang through his ears in a tunnel of mindless noise. He nodded, the chute jerked open and Firefreak burst into action.

Tighe stared up at the arena ceiling, shocked to find himself on his back. A bullfighter yelled, helped guide him in a headlong rush to the corral side as Tighe gasped from the pain flooding his leg. Firefreak danced a wild jig of triumph before being chased from the ring.

Tighe glanced at the time.

Three seconds. He'd made it three seconds.

And he was pretty certain he'd done something to his leg. Heat and white-hot pain shot up to his groin. Worse, he'd proved his family right—in front of River.

"Are you all right, Tighe?" River asked, suddenly at his side as Galen checked him over.

Tighe stumbled toward a bench and let his brothers help him out of his gear. "I'm fine. Nothing damaged but my pride."

"And his leg," Galen announced. "Brother, you're going to be bed-bound for a while."

"I'm fine." Tighe was bothered that he hadn't had the epiphany he'd been expecting while on Firefreak.

True, Dante had been known to exaggerate—and maybe he'd even told a wee fib just to goad Tighe on. But Dante had sworn to his siblings that for the few seconds he'd been on that bull, he'd been absolutely, mindlessly free of his demons.

"You're not fine." Galen moved a practiced hand over his leg, divining what would take other doctors X-rays to learn. "You have a fracture, brother. And a groin tear. You'll be out of commission a good six weeks."

"And we were already shorthanded," Ashlyn said, not sparing words as his other siblings grouped around him. "You'll have to learn to take care of yourself from your bed. None of us can give up ranch duties to tend you, when we told you that riding Firefreak was practically a death wish for you."

He wasn't the big zero on the back of a bull they thought he was. "I'll be fine." He looked at River, saw the worry on her face, tried to smile reassuringly. "I am fine."

"I'll nurse him." She looked at him, then around at his siblings. "Goodness knows he's a pain, but I can bring the twins and watch all three of them."

"Three children," Ash said. "Somehow seems fitting." She glared at her brother.

"You guys can be as annoyed as you want," Tighe said. "As soon as I'm healed, I'm getting right back on that ornery son of a gun."

"He hit his head." Jace shook his own numskull, not understanding his brother's determination. "You must have, or you wouldn't say something so dumb."

"I'm getting back on him," Tighe repeated, "Firefreak is a pussycat."

"Maybe you can talk some sense into my intelligence-challenged brother," Ash whispered to River.

Tighe smiled. Dante said that riding Firefreak had brought him closer to Ana, and now River was going to take care of him while he was bed-bound.

Firefreak's the best thing that ever happened to me. "Awesome," Tighe said, swallowing back a slight moan as Galen and Jace began fitting a board to his leg so they could get him to a hospital. Tighe winked at River, the woman to whom he'd made love last night—sweet as an angel—the only woman worth pulling his groin over just to get her attention.

AFTER A TRIP to the hospital and then a visit to an orthopedist that didn't do much for his mental state, which at the moment was black and aggrieved, Tighe sat in Jace's truck, his leg up on the backseat, thrilled to be going home. The seven-chimney, Tudor-style mansion that Molly and Jeremiah Callahan had built long ago to house their young family of six sturdy Callahan boys—the Chacon Callahans' cousins—rose like a beautiful postcard from its New Mexico grounds. Backed by panoramic spools of canyons and gorges, Rancho Diablo was an amazing sight. Tighe didn't think he'd ever get over the breathtaking beauty of the ranch. He'd been born and raised in the Chacon tribe, then served in the military, where life was a whole lot different than here. He loved the ranch and the small town of Diablo, loved being with his family, enjoying a new closeness they hadn't been able to share in many years. Even the constant threat of danger couldn't always rub the shine off Rancho Diablo's surroundings.

But the truck didn't turn toward the main house, and Tighe's radar went on alert. "Why are you taking me to Sloan and Kendall's house?" Something was most certainly afoot.

"Since River has agreed to be your nurse—I can't imagine why—" Ash said, "Kendall says it would be best for you to be here. This way River can keep an eye on all her charges. It'll be better if the twins' normal schedule isn't interrupted."

This didn't sound good at all. "Much as I love my little nephews," Tighe said, "I don't want to stay at Sloan and Kendall's. I'll stay in my own room in the bunkhouse." How could he ever be alone with River if he was sharing space with little Carlos and Isaiah? They were active, trying to pull themselves up on unsteady feet, eager to find their range and explore.

There would be no time for romancing the tall, delicious bodyguard with two busy rug rats taking up her every second. "Not to be selfish or anything," he said, and Ash said, "Go ahead and admit it, you're selfish. I can hear the wheels turning in your head. 'How can I be alone with River if I'm laid up with my darling nephews?'" she added in a high voice, mimicking what she thought he was thinking, and in fact, what he had been thinking.

"I am selfish." Tighe sighed. "Something's happened to me. I used to be footloose and, well, footloose."

"Now it's just your head that's loose. Come on, brother. Let me help you inside." Ash hopped out, opened his door.

He glared at her. "No. Take me to the bunkhouse, or the main house. I would rather suffer in silence than be just another—"

"Helpless person River has to keep an eye on?" Ash prodded.

"The trouble is, you don't suffer in silence. Come on." Jace put his shoulder under Tighe's to give him support as he unsteadily maneuvered himself out of the truck. "You're lucky we don't just leave you out in the peacock pens to heal, where we can't hear you moan and groan."

It was too humiliating. He wouldn't look like a warrior, wouldn't be a hero with badass courageous qualities if his woman tossed him in with the kiddies as an extra responsibility.

"Either you take me to the bunkhouse or I'm going to the canyons." After making fierce love to that little lady practically all night long, he wasn't about to appear anything less than a stud—and he couldn't be that if he was laid out on a sofa. "The weather's fine. The canyons suit me just as well as anywhere."

"Be a sitting duck for Uncle Wolf and his cretinous crew," Jace said. "Come on, be practical, bro."

Jace didn't understand practical. Practical was when you could think past the sirens that screamed in your head every time the woman you had a thing for got within ten feet. Tighe had lost his practicality a long time ago. "Canyons or bunkhouse. Take your pick. Can't promise to stay either place."

Ash sighed. "Flip a coin. Either decision is bad. Fiona will roost on the bunkhouse if you stay there, she'll be so worried that you're an easy mark. The canyons and you're even more of a sitting duck."

That sounded very much like conditions he'd lived under in Afghanistan. He could survive there by his wits, and wouldn't be taking up any of the family's time. Tighe brightened. "The canyons. Who's riding canyon right now?"

"You were supposed to," Jace said sourly. "It was

your shift. Now Xav Phillips says he'll come back and take over, which isn't a good idea." Jace glanced at Ash, who was talking on a cell phone to River, complaining that Tighe was a stubborn ass. "We don't need Xav in the canyons, dude, as you well know, because Ash will find a thousand reasons and ways to get down there to haunt her favorite cowboy."

"Who's got a favorite cowboy?" Ash asked, returning. "Apparently, not River right now. She's annoyed with you, Tighe." Ash grinned. "She says you have to go to Sloan's, because she can't leave the twins to visit you in the bunkhouse."

Even better. He didn't want River around while he healed. A lightning flash of intuition told him he'd be better off returning when he was all better, a hero again—not the poor sap everyone was annoyed with. "Really, I'm such a pain in the ass, the only place I can be is the canyons."

"I agree completely. Still, a bad idea," Jace said.

"But—" Ash began, and Tighe waved her to silence.

"I've made up my mind." What use was he as a man if he was on par with the twins? "I got myself into this mess and I'll get myself out. As a matter of fact, just take me to the stone and fire ring. All I need is a bottle of whiskey and some girlie mags. I'll be fine."

Ash and Jace stared at him, their expressions dismayed.

"Okay, no girlie mags," Tighe said, loving messing with his siblings. They thought he wasn't big and bad right now. Well, he was; he was a monster pain in the butt, and that was just the way a man should be.

"You'll be unprotected," Ash said. "Much as you're the only one among us with such disregard for yourself, you still do not want to put yourself out there with a bull's-eye on you for Wolf and his gang. Listen to me," she pleaded. "I'll worry myself sick."

"Sick about what?" River asked.

The three Callahans stared at the tall woman who'd just walked up, catching the last words of their conversation. Just the sight of that gorgeous creature made his blood pound. River gave him the wild, mad dreams of a man who'd tasted heaven once and was determined to do it again. Once he was healed, he was coming back for her.

"Nobody's worried about a thing," Tighe said.

"I'm worried." Ash looked at River for help. "My jackass of a brother wants to camp out in the open instead of stay in the house with you and the twins. In the *open*," she emphasized.

River didn't miss Ash's message. She met his gaze, didn't look away. Peered deep inside him, until he felt her reaching into his soul.

The woman practically stole his very breath.

"I'll drive you out there," River said.

Chapter Three

After he'd packed up some gear and run the gauntlet of a protesting aunt Fiona and family, River hustled Tighe into the military jeep and steered it toward the canyons. He glanced over at the goddess next to him, trying to decipher the change in her mood. She certainly wasn't the cooing, sexy tigress he'd had in his arms last night.

He'd have to call River's mood elusive, which didn't sit well with him at all. It almost felt as if she was abandoning him without a thought.

"Thanks for the ride. My siblings weren't going to bring me."

Glossy dark strands of hair blew around her face as she drove, rather speedily, he thought, given the uneven terrain. She could at least quit mashing the pedal.

"It's not my worry if you've got a death wish. I have no desire to keep you from your fondest desires, Tighe."

That didn't sound right. *She* was his fondest desire. "I don't have a death wish."

"Don't you?" She leveled him with brown eyes that held not a care in them. "First Firefreak. Now sleeping in the open, when you know that the ranch has been under siege for forever. For longer than either you or I have even been here."

Aw, she was fretting about him, the cute little thing. He reached over and gave her shoulder an affectionate squeeze.

She batted away his hand. His brows rose. "Regretting last night?"

She turned to him, her forehead pinched in a frown. "Regretting what?"

He hardly knew what to say, since this darling angel seemed to have suddenly sprouted a ten-inch layer of cactus needles around herself. "You and me."

"Hardly," she shot back. "It didn't mean a thing, cowboy."

He tried not to let his jaw fall open. "Nothing?"

"Should it have?"

It certainly had to him. Hell, he'd gotten on Firefreak for her! Making love to her, plus facing his greatest challenge since coming to Diablo—well, it was the greatest cocktail of adrenaline and gut-punching life he'd ever experienced. "You know me. It's just all about getting naked," he bragged, trying to sound like his old self, the self he'd been before they'd made love. His whole world had changed—shouldn't hers have, too?

"Where am I dropping you off?"

She sounded completely unworried. Tighe comforted himself that that was because everyone knew he could take care of himself. "At the stone ring, please."

At that news, she did look a little alarmed. "You'll be out in the open. I think your family assumes you're at least taking shelter in one of the caves or overhangs."

"Wouldn't do any good. Wolf will find me if he wants to, and frankly, I don't care if he does."

"You're injured, Tighe. I know you don't like to

admit to mortality, but you do recall that seven goons tied up your sister and Xav Phillips just last month?"

Tighe had no intention of hanging out in a cave like a cowering dog, away from the stars he loved and the fresh breezes that stirred his soul. "It's just a little groin pull, darling. No worries. However," he said, perking up, "maybe you'd like to hang around and nurse my groi—"

"And a hairline fracture," River interrupted.

"I mend best in the open. I lived in the tribe. Was deployed to some hellish places. Don't you worry about me, beautiful."

"I'm not," she snapped. "I think you're an idiot."

Well, that wasn't how a man wanted the angel of his dreams to view him. "Harsh."

"Honest."

She pulled up to the stone ring. Large rocks, one set for each of the seven Chacon Callahans, encircled a small glowing fire. His grandfather, Chief Running Bear, tended the blaze. The chief said this place was their home now, while they protected Callahan land, and the mystical black Diablos, the spirit horses that lived in the canyons. They were the true wealth of Rancho Diablo.

"Home sweet home," Tighe said.

"Then get out," River said, "if this is where you want to be."

He turned to look at her. "Gorgeous, I'm pretty sure I showed you a good time in bed. Is there a reason you're all prickly suddenly?"

She met his gaze. "I told you. I'm pretty sure you're the loose cannon I always believed you were."

He winced internally. This was true. But it wasn't necessary to rub in the fact that he'd clearly failed to change her mind. "All right, sweet face. Try not to miss me too much," he said, getting out of the jeep and managing his crutches a bit more slowly and painfully than his jaunty tone implied.

"I won't miss you at all." She wheeled the jeep around and drove away, apparently not even curious as to where he planned to lay his bedroll.

"Guess that means we won't be sharing the old pillow tonight. It's a shame, because I'm pretty sure you're kidding yourself, my hottie bodyguard." He hobbled around, trying to find a place to settle, not altogether surprised when his grandfather appeared.

"Howdy, Chief." Tighe tossed his bedroll down. "Haven't seen you since Dante's wedding."

"I've seen you." Running Bear picked up the bedroll. "Come."

Tighe followed as fast as his crutches would allow. "Where are we headed?"

The chief disappeared behind some thick cacti. A threadlike stream encircled a wide stone dugout tucked back and hidden so well that Tighe would never have seen it even if he'd been looking for it. He had a feeling his brothers and Ash had no idea about Running Bear's lair. Well, Ashlyn might; she seemed to know more than most. But he thought Galen, Jace, Falcon, his pinheaded twin, Dante, and Sloan were just as in the dark as he was. "Nice digs, Grandfather."

Running Bear grunted. Tighe felt honored that his grandfather had brought him to his private sanctuary. They sat near the opening, staring out over the curling canyons below. "Wow, this is quite a view."

"Yes." Running Bear didn't look at him as Tighe gingerly settled himself against the rock ledge so his leg could jut forward for support. "We need to discuss your time at Rancho Diablo."

"My time?"

His grandfather gazed out into the distance. Sudden fear clenched Tighe's gut. The old chief had warned the seven Chacon Callahans that one of them was the hunted one, the one who would bring harm to the family. Was it *him?* Was that why Running Bear had brought him here? Somehow Tighe had known this was where he belonged, almost from the moment he'd realized River had gone chilly on him.

"Tell me what I should do, Grandfather," he said, and the old man closed his eyes, though Tighe knew he wasn't dozing.

"Meditate on who you are," Running Bear said. "You are not yet who you will be."

Tighe didn't know how to be anything other than what he was. Some—like River—claimed he was a bit wild. Maybe he was. Certainly he liked to live on the edge, but wasn't that part of enjoying life to the max? His family teased him, calling him more taciturn than his talkative twin, but that had been when they were kids. The military had thought he was fairly accurate and single-minded when it came to sniper skills. Tighe had earned the moniker Takedown. He'd liked living almost alone at times, when he was on an assignment. Other times he'd appreciated the camaraderie and brotherhood of his platoon. It had been a close bond, reminiscent of his tribe. "Chief, I don't know how to be anything different than what I am."

His grandfather looked at him. "You will learn."

Then he left the stone crevasse, disappearing without a sound. Tighe leaned back against the rough wall with a sigh. He looked out over the canyons from his grandfather's aerie, and wondered if he would ever get River to kiss him again. She seemed to think he needed to change somehow, too.

He was pretty resistant to that. "Twenty-seven years of being the opposite of Dante wasn't so bad," he muttered. "I'd rather be me than him."

He liked being wild and free. What exactly was wrong with that?

Even River wouldn't want him to change that much. She had to have liked him the way he was or she wouldn't have allowed him to make love to her.

Then again, he could consider changing just a little if she'd open her arms to him again. Problem was, he didn't know what he was supposed to change. Tighe closed his eyes, willed himself to meditate.

"Every journey changes your soul. Each journey is a path to self-knowledge," Running Bear said. "There is no life without this."

"I know, Grandfather, I know. I remember your teachings." Tighe opened his eyes, glanced around. Running Bear was nowhere to be seen. But his words remained in Tighe's mind, delicate as air.

Closing his eyes again, he allowed the mysticism he knew so well to envelop him, something he hadn't done in a long, long time.

"WHAT ARE YOU DOING?" Ash asked River, who was looking out a window in the main house, toward the barn. River had specifically chosen this room for her project.

"I'm spying on your brothers. And Sawyer. There's something strange about her. I don't believe for a second that she's had real training as a bodyguard. Not like Ana and I had."

"The little twins seem to like her."

"Isaiah and Carlos like her because they're Callahan males. They're predisposed to like pretty girls from the moment they're conceived. That doesn't make her a bodyguard. It makes her a decent nanny. Maybe."

Ash flopped into a chair. "When I asked Kendall why she'd hired Storm Cash's niece, she said Sawyer had the right training, and that she'd spent time in the desert honing her skills. Kendall said she checked her background, and Sawyer and Storm hadn't been close during Sawyer's childhood. So in Kendall's maternal opinion, there was no reason to eliminate a perfectly good bodyguard just because of some stinky family relations. And Kendall said sometimes it was best to keep your enemies tucked tight to one's bosom."

"I like my bosom enemy-free. I'm not leaving until I know the twins are in capable hands," River stated.

Ash watched Sawyer below, chatting up Jace, as little Isaiah and Carlos happily sat in their double stroller. "I didn't know you were planning on leaving. And yet, I guess I did know. I was just hoping my hunch was wrong." Ash sighed. "You're going to find Tighe, aren't you?"

"It's time someone does." It had been three weeks since she'd driven Tighe to the stone fire ring. She had no idea what he was eating or drinking, or if he was miserable from his leg injury. None of the Callahans, including the protective aunt Fiona, seemed all that worried. When River had mentioned to Fiona that maybe her husband, Burke, might need to go check on Tighe, she had shaken her head and said she didn't have time for such monkeyshines.

"Oh, Tighe's fine. Don't worry about him. When he was a boy—"

River glanced at Ash, who seemed to suddenly have swallowed her words. "When he was a boy, what?"

"I was just going to say that once when we were young, Tighe went off for a while. I was six," Ash said, "so I remember it well." She smiled at River. "It's all right. We're used to him being independent."

"If you were six, Tighe was eight when he went on this adventure. How long was he gone?" River was curious as to how he had fared in his childhood. "Five, six hours?"

"Two months," Ash said softly. "He was gone two months, in the coldest part of the year. Most of us wanted to stay close to the fire at night. Tighe wanted to find out if he could build his own fire and survive on what he found and caught."

River sucked in her breath. "No parent would allow that."

"Oh." Ash shook her head, got up. "No worries about that. Tighe was never really alone, though he doesn't know that, so don't tell him. It would totally crush him and blow his wild man conception of himself. But there were always scouts watching him. Not that the scouts would have interfered, unless there'd been severe danger. A test is a test, and Tighe wanted the chance to test himself." Ash fluffed her silvery-blond, shoulder-length hair, not concerned in the least. "Grandfather said Tighe had the soul of a tiger, and that he would make many kills when he left the tribe. And he did. He was a pretty good sniper. Don't worry about my pinheaded brother," she said. "He's more wolf than man. Tighe's problem is that is he's scared, maybe for the first time in his life."

"Scared of what? Not rattlesnakes, or becoming a

dried-out skeleton, with no food or water in the canyons."

"My guess is," Ash said, "he's been a little scared ever since you came here."

"Me?"

"Maybe. Tighe's always seen himself as the uncatchable male. Also, I think it's come to his mind that he might be the hunted one."

"You know," River said, looking back out the window, "it could be you, Ash."

She shook her head. "Not me. But if it is, I hope someone shoots me and puts me out of my misery."

"Shoots you?" River was horrified. "Who would do that?"

"I'm hoping you," Ash said softly, looking at her. "You've always got your Beretta strapped to your thigh, don't you?"

"I would never shoot you," River snapped. "And how do you know about my gun?"

"I know everything," Ash said, wandering out the door.

"I see," River muttered, watching Sawyer stretch up to kiss Jace on the cheek on the ground below her second-story window. "Really nice to know I've fallen for some kind of hard-core survivalist wolf-man. And that woman is working an angle," she said of Sawyer, watching her slink off, leaving a seemingly stunned Jace behind. "Don't fall for it, handsome."

Jace would probably fall like a ton of bricks. She watched Jace almost strut, all peacocklike, his gaze fastened on Sawyer's backside. River sighed and got up from her perch. Ash's wealth of information had unsettled her to some degree. Tighe wasn't afraid of her—not in the least. That could be ruled out. He was stubborn and opinioned, but not afraid of a woman.

Now the other business…was he the hunted one? Ash was crazy if she thought River was going to shoot her, if it turned out to be her. "The only shooting I'm doing is at bad guys, and there may not be any of those," River said, watching Jace rub his cheek where Sawyer had pecked him. "Just gullible ones."

She went to hunt up Tighe, the resident wolf on the loose.

THE STONE CIRCLE showed few signs of anyone living there, though a small fire flickered, the embers glowing. There were no signs of foul play, but River felt uneasiness in the pit of her stomach. A man with a sore groin and a fractured leg should be right here where she'd left him.

"Hello, beautiful," she heard someone say, and River turned.

"What are you doing?" she demanded. "Why are you standing up?"

Tighe smiled, feeling very much in control of the situation, obviously, by the devilish light in his eyes. "You were worried about me."

"No, I wasn't." Why add to his already overburdened ego?

"You were." He stumped forward, resting his weight on a crutch crudely fashioned from the forked limb of a tree. "I'm glad you were worried about me, but I could have told you there was no need."

"Then I'll be going." She didn't feel like putting up with his macho attitude when he'd worried her half to death for days. "I'll let your family know you're fine."

"I may return with you for a bit. You got room in your ride?"

She'd driven the military jeep, which had plenty of space for cargo. "I suppose."

He got in without needing assistance and grinned at her. "Unless you want a tour, I'm ready to head back."

She looked at the cowboy, the man who invaded her dreams and kept her breathless whenever she thought about him. "Are you sure this is what you want?"

"For the moment. That's how I live—I'm totally in the moment." He grinned, pleased with his lone-wolf persona.

She gazed at his rangy body, and his long hair, which hadn't seen much of a brush in the three weeks he'd been gone. He looked as delectable as ever. It was annoying that a man could hunker in the wilderness and not suffer ill effects. "I have to admit I was afraid of what I'd find."

"You don't think I can live without Fiona's cookies." Tighe laughed. "I miss the comforts of home, but mostly the children, I have to admit." He caught her hand as she put it on the shift. "Sometimes I even missed you."

"Did you?" She shifted, moving his hand away. "I didn't miss you a bit."

It was a lie, of course, to save face.

"I think you did," he said cheerfully. "But I understand you want to keep it to yourself. It was sweet of you to come find me. I'm surprised my family didn't tell you there was nothing to worry about."

He was so annoying she wanted to dump him out of the jeep. The thing was, everything he was teasing her about was true—she *had* missed him, and she *had* worried. Did anything ever get under his skin? "Hey, fun fact," River said, "I've skipped my period."

Oh, for a photo of Tighe's expression. He looked… stunned. River kept driving, curious to see what he'd say, pretty pleased that she'd found the one thing that would shut him up for just a moment.

A loud whoop erupted from him. Tighe threw his straw Resistol into the air and laughed out loud, loudly enough to startle birds from trees, if there'd been any around.

Apparently he wasn't so much the silent type as his siblings had claimed.

"That's awesome! When will we know for certain? How long do these things take?"

"In a couple of weeks I'll go to the doctor. I keep telling myself maybe I'm late because of worrying—"

"About me—"

"No. About things at the ranch," River interrupted, "but I've always been completely regular."

"You cute little thing," Tighe said. "That night you and my brother and sister were plotting against me, you had your own little plot going."

"Not hardly." River was getting mad. "Perhaps you didn't do a decent job wrapping up."

"You helped, as I recall," he said gleefully, "and I remember you seemed to be impressed."

"Oh, for crying out loud." River parked the jeep at the house, jumped down. "You can just wait there until one of your siblings finds you. Or Wolf. Right now, I don't care."

She went inside, aggravated beyond belief.

"Did you find my brother?" Jace asked.

"I found a jackass. It might have been your brother. You can go out to the jeep and see for yourself."

With that, she went to check on the twins.

Chapter Four

"Whew. What'd you say to River to get her in a knot?" Jace asked, as Tighe helped himself down from the jeep, still grinning from ear to ear.

"That amazing woman is highly annoyed because she's caught herself a man."

"Who?" Jace glanced around. "Why is that annoying? Don't women want a man like a bee wants a flower?"

"Yes, they do. They just don't want to admit it." Tighe's heart was singing. "There's a good chance I'm going to be a father." He laughed, pleased.

"How did that happen?" Jace frowned. "You mean you may have gotten River in a family way?"

"I think she got me in a family way. As I recall, the two of you plotted against me. I just fell willingly into the trap." He went inside to hit the cookie tray and gloat.

"What are you going to do?" Jace sat down at the kitchen counter next to him. "I don't envision you settling down."

"I didn't say a word about settling down." Tighe munched on a sugar cookie. "She didn't say anything about that, either." He looked at his brother. "We'll know for sure in a couple of weeks, but I know now what the spirits were trying to tell me. I'm definitely going to be a dad." He let out a wolf howl, bringing Fiona into the kitchen.

"Mercy!" She glared at her nephew. "I thought a wild animal got into the house!"

"One did. My brother," Jace said drily. "He thinks he's going to be a father."

Fiona's jaw dropped. "A father? Weren't you supposed to be on a wilderness sabbatical, resting and considering the stars?"

"It's what he did *before* the sabbatical," Jace explained, and Tighe reached out to hug his aunt.

"I have you to thank, Aunt Fiona. If you hadn't been so determined to keep me from my destiny—"

"Your destiny?" She frowned.

"Firefreak," Tighe said reverently. "You sent an angel to keep me from my destiny, and my destiny was the angel. What a wise aunt you are."

"Yes, well," Fiona said, her voice uncertain. "You sound like you have dehydration symptoms and perhaps starvation issues. I'll put in a meat loaf."

She crossed the kitchen and pulled out some pans, not proffering him the excited congratulations Tighe thought he'd earned. "Aren't you excited that there will be another Callahan tot around, Aunt Fiona?"

She looked at him as she unwrapped some meat. "I'll have to talk to River."

"My baby mama is going to be beautiful when she's in full bloom," Tighe said, very satisfied. "I'm going to love being a dad."

"You're going to have to figure out a way to get her to the altar then," Fiona said.

"Piece of cake."

"That's what you'd been saying for the past year, that you had River all wrapped up," Jace pointed out. "But then we figured out she didn't have a boyfriend in Tempest, that she was just trying to stay away from you. And just because she slept with you once doesn't mean she's inclined to do it again. Especially since you showed deficient skills at simple tasks, like wearing a—"

"I have plenty of skill, thanks." Tighe got up. "I'm going to go find her. You doubters will see, the woman is crazy about me. She's just a little shy, doesn't want to seem too eager about catching her a Callahan cowboy. But I like her eager," he said, remembering the night he'd made love to her. "In fact, if you don't see me again tonight, don't come looking for me."

"Best of luck," Jace said, and Fiona flapped a dish towel his way, shooing him off.

He didn't need luck. He had what his little lady liked—and it had nothing to do with luck.

"Go away," River told Tighe when he walked into Sloan and Kendall's house. She was playing with the twins, about to start their baths. "If you're here to talk to me, I'm not in the mood."

"Don't be prickly, beautiful. You and I have things to discuss. Hey, boys." He ruffled the hair on Carlos and Isaiah's heads, a fond uncle, even if he was still gimping around and not able to get down and play with them the way he liked.

River put away the toys. "I've thought long and hard about this, and if we're going to be parents, you're going to have to do this my way."

"Meaning?"

"Separately. Just because Falcon and Sloan and Dante got together with their—"

"Baby mamas?" Tighe said helpfully.

"I really don't like that expression. How about mother of your child?" River said.

"Kinda formal, don't you think?"

She refused to look at the handsome cowboy who might be bound to her forever now. "Let's not discuss it more until we know for certain. I don't have any intention of tying you down."

"That's fine," Tighe said, "I'll do the tying down, sweetheart, if there's tying to be done."

Her body seemed to lighten and expand at his words. Her friend Ana had mentioned that Dante had been forthright in his pursuit of her, and that she didn't expect Tighe to be any different.

River didn't want to be pursued, and she wasn't certain how to get that through his head—or hers. She'd felt the unmistakable surge of excitement at the thought of being romanced by him. When he'd made love to her, it had been like magic, pure magic, and she'd adored every minute of it.

"You know you want me," Tighe said, his voice teasing, and River looked at him, and thought, *Yes, I do. But it's just not going to happen.*

"THIS IS SO going to happen," Tighe said, following River to her room. "We need to get to know each other much better since we're going to be parents."

"We don't know for sure."

"I know for sure. And I can't wait. Pack up your stuff, doll face. I need a night nurse."

"You need nothing and no one. I have this on good authority from your sister."

River wouldn't even look at him, the cute, shy little thing. "Don't listen to Ash," Tighe told her. "She thinks she's the family font of all knowledge, but we humored her growing up. She was sheltered, babied. She doesn't know a thing." He settled on River's bed. "I can't sleep here with you. It wouldn't be appropriate for the twins."

"Yes, I know," River said sweetly, but he wasn't fooled in the least.

"You'll have to be my night nurse at the bunkhouse."

"If you need a nurse, ask Fiona. I have a job. In fact, my job is the exact reason why nothing further is going to happen between you and me."

He frowned, not liking the sound of that.

"The thing is, it's unprofessional. In fact, it was unprofessional, what I did with you," River said, her cheeks turning a becoming pink Tighe thought was adorable. "I shouldn't have allowed your aunt and family to talk me into that little adventure, and I should have…turned you away when you came to my room that night."

He laughed. She was just such a sexy fireball. "Sweetcakes, you wouldn't have turned me away. As I recall, you scooted over and made room for me in that tiny little bed."

Her face went bright red. He grinned. "I liked it. Made me feel very welcome. And that's what I'm going to do for you tonight, when you come to my bed."

"I won't be doing any such thing," she said, a little snappishly, but he wasn't afraid of a girl with spirit.

Tighe got to his feet. "See you later."

"I don't think so."

He headed out the door to the bunkhouse. He'd be seeing River all right—the lady liked him.

But not as much as he liked her.
Give me time. I'll change her mind.

TIGHE HEARD HIS door open about midnight, and smiled in the darkness. This was awesome. He'd known River would come. She couldn't resist him. Whether she wanted to admit it or not, they shared something special. He pretended to be asleep, so he wouldn't ruin her surprise.

He'd act so surprised, and then make love to her until she admitted she was crazy about him.

The light flipped on, jarring his eyes open. River stood there, wearing a robe and high-heeled slippers. He grinned. "Well, hello, gorgeous. Come to nurse me back to a full-strength wild man?"

He watched her move his crutch away from his nightstand, a bit out of his reach. Of course, he wouldn't need that tonight. River gave him a long gaze, then opened her robe, and he swallowed so hard he thought he might choke. Not a scrap was on her body.

"Holy smokes," he said, "come to Daddy. And don't take the long route. Jump right into my arms."

River closed her robe.

He looked at her. "If you're cold, I'll be happy to warm you, darling."

She gave him one last look, took his crutch and left the room.

"That little devil. What was that all about?" He hobbled out of his room, glanced around the bunkhouse. His nocturnal angel had gone, taking all the sexy joy away.

Now he was stiff in several places.

"That little lady and I have got to work some things

out," he muttered, and climbed back into bed, completely disgruntled.

And then he got it. She was trying to drive him mad. That was the plan, while he was in no shape to give proper chase. She was going to make him crazy, make him want her, until he begged her to be his woman.

"No, YOU DOPE," Jace said the next day when Tighe mentioned that he'd had the strangest dream in the night, wherein River had nearly killed him with a vision of divine beauty, then cruelly snatched it away. "She's not softening toward you. I heard Ash and her discussing it. She was showing you how cruel it had been that you sandbagged her in her hotel room that night. Ash told her you had to realize that what happens in the night doesn't necessarily translate to real life. Sort of what happens in Vegas stays in Vegas."

"My sister put my girlfriend up to giving me a relationship lesson? Isn't that the blind leading the blind?" Now that he understood what had happened, Tighe felt a whole lot better. It explained the wild look in her big eyes, as if she wasn't totally committed to the caper, perhaps might have even been nervous.

"I wouldn't put it so harshly. Ladies cook up these plans all the time. Guys do, too, but we're more interested in getting into ladies' drawers than staying out of them. River wants you to know that the two of you don't have anything that translates to real life." Jace kicked back in the bunkhouse, grinned at his brother. "This one's gonna be tough, bro. And you've only got one leg to chase her on."

"Won't matter." Tighe felt a bit deflated suddenly. Maybe River didn't want him. Was that possible?

Nah. No way.

"Hey, give me a ride, will you?" he asked Jace.

"Heading back to the canyons?"

"No. Not yet." He stumped toward the jeep. There was only one place to go when a woman was on the fence about a man, and if a man was smart, he got himself there and did the thing right. Big. Huge.

He could do impressive.

"This isn't a good idea," Ash said, poking her nose into his business as she loved to do. "What message did you not receive during her midnight visit? What happens at night isn't real life, bro."

"Why did you come with me to Diablo, anyway?" Tighe muttered, wondering if his sister was right as he stared into the jewelry case at all the twinkling engagement rings. He was suddenly doubtful, and Ash wasn't helping.

"You don't even know if River's having your child," Jace pointed out. "This is premature. Maybe."

"I want River to know that, baby or no baby, I want to marry her. Whatever happens, I'm the man she wants."

"I don't think so," Ash said. "Not that I'm trying to knock your good leg out from underneath you, but I'm pretty sure she hasn't changed her mind about you."

Tighe shook his head. "She has a great poker face." And a great body, but he forbore adding that.

"She's not faking it," Ash told him. "I believe in my heart that River thinks a real relationship isn't built on nighttime shenanigans."

"I'll take that one," he said to the jeweler, pointing to the biggest sparkler in the case. "Bigger is always better."

Ash sighed. "Your head is bigger than most men's, and that's not better."

"True," Jace said. "Why don't you wait another month, so you don't crowd her? You know how sometimes if you try to rush an animal, it goes in the opposite direction?"

Tighe debated whether he was getting good advice from his siblings. If he was, it would be the first time.

"Since our family came here to Rancho Diablo," he said softly, "we've changed. All of us have worked hard. We've done what Running Bear wanted us to do. The mission was understood, and we've kept to it. But River is outside of the mission. And she makes my heart whole. That's the only way I know how to explain it."

Ash nodded. "I know. But we were just trying to keep you off of Firefreak," she said gently. "We didn't expect that the plot would go as far as it appears it did."

He swallowed hard. "River didn't sleep with me to keep me off a bull. Nothing and nobody could have kept me from that ride."

"I know." Ash sighed. "Never mind. Forget I said anything."

Tighe looked at the ring he'd selected with some regret. "Maybe you're right."

"Probably this once, she is," Jace said. "You hate to jump the gun. Ladies can be so giddy."

"Not really," Ash said. "We're just practical. We can see the forest for the trees. We can—"

"Come on," Tighe said. "Drive me back, Sophocles."

He felt a bit roughed up and heartbroken. No man wanted to think a woman wouldn't be thrilled with his proposal and a beautiful ring. But Ash knew River better than he did. Feeling like a dog with a tucked tail,

Tighe allowed his brother and sister to usher him out of the jewelry store.

By the jeep stood their uncle Wolf, grinning at them with his typical up-to-no-good grimace. Tighe wished he wasn't using a crutch, hated to appear weak in front of the enemy. "Look what the summer wind blew in. Pollution."

"Well, if it isn't my favorite family members," Wolf said.

"Spare us," Ash said, getting into the jeep. "When are you going to give up? We're not going anywhere. Rancho Diablo is our home."

"Just wanted to warn you that we saw some strange things in the canyons, me and my men." Wolf looked at them. "Might have been some birds of prey. Never can be sure at a distance."

"What are you getting at?" Tighe demanded.

"Have you checked on Running Bear lately?"

Tighe settled into the back of the jeep, and Jace got in the passenger seat while Ash switched on the engine. "No one needs to check on the chief. He checks on everyone, including you. Even black sheep get watched by the shepherd."

Wolf's expression turned peeved, though he shrugged. "Just a thought." He walked away, went inside the Books'n'Bingo Society bookshop and tearoom. Up the main street, Tighe saw a few of Wolf's merry stragglers staring them down.

"I've got a bad feeling about this," he said under his breath.

"So do I," Ash murmured. "For one thing, Wolf's gone into Fiona's tearoom, which means he plans to stir up trouble. But that bit about Running Bear—"

"Is a trap," Jace said.

"Agreed. Head for home." Tighe shoved his hat low on his head, settled his leg more comfortably, trying to ignore the sudden yawing pit in his stomach. No one could get to Running Bear; their grandfather was part of the canyons and the wind and the sun.

They knew Running Bear wasn't immortal. He just seemed like it.

Closing his eyes, Tighe tried to envision his grandfather as Ash sped toward Rancho Diablo. Searched his mind for the old chief's spirit.

Something didn't feel quite right. He just couldn't put his finger on it.

It felt as if change was coming.

THE RANCH WAS alive with women when Tighe returned with his siblings. Ladies of all shapes and sizes filed into the house, carrying bags and boxes and notebooks.

"Wow." Ash parked the jeep, staring. "Has Aunt Fiona got one of her meetings today?"

Jace grunted. "Looks like every woman in Diablo is here. Maybe she forgot to tell everyone the meeting is at the Books'n'Bingo tearoom, as they always are."

Tighe got down out of the vehicle, ignoring his brother's help. "I've got a crutch," he snapped. "Anyway, my leg is almost healed."

"Not until Galen examines it and says so. No heroics. We've had enough of those." Jace headed toward the house with Ash, leaving Tighe to stump along behind.

Inside, the ladies were an excited gaggle of happy faces and energetic voices. His aunt was in her element in the middle of the crowd Tighe estimated to be somewhere around thirty. He kissed her on the cheek.

"Aunt Fiona, did you forget to send me an invitation to the party?"

River stood nearby, gorgeous but not pleased, if he gauged her mood correctly. She wasn't smiling, though to be fair, she was beautiful even when she frowned. "I sure do have a thing for you," he said to her, and she shook her head and drifted into another room.

"What's going on, Aunt Fiona?"

"I think you better talk things over with River," Fiona said.

His heart fell into his boots.

"You always were the unpredictable one," his aunt said with a grin.

"Oh, no, Aunt Fiona, this baby shower isn't for River, is it?" River already had a tiny touch of cold feet. This wouldn't help. He strode out of the room to follow her.

"River?" She was putting some small, crustless sandwiches on a tray in the kitchen. "What's going on?"

"Well," River said, "apparently we're definitely pregnant."

His heart leaped for joy. Yet she wasn't smiling, so he sensed a heartfelt "Hurray!" wasn't appropriate. "And Aunt Fiona already planned a baby shower?"

She shook her head. "This isn't for me, although the word is definitely out and plans are in full swing. I'm surprised you weren't mobbed with congratulations when you walked into the house."

He glanced over his shoulder to where the women were corralled in the den, chatting. "You could have called and let me know. I'd have liked to be first and not last."

"Don't worry. This is just a planning meeting for

the upcoming Christmas ball." River handed him the tray. "Six months is hardly enough time for Fiona to get everything done she wants, so the planning must begin now. Volunteers must be pressed into work, committees formed."

"Yes, yes," Tighe said, impatient, "but what did the doctor say?"

River shrugged. "That I'm healthy. The pregnancy is right where it should be, considering."

He frowned. River really wasn't happy about carrying his child. Somehow he was going to have to fix this. "That's good. We'll get you on some good prenatal vitamins, make sure you get lots of rest...." He glanced out at his aunt, who had called her committee to order. "It's quite a coincidence that Fiona gathered all these ladies on the spur of the moment, just for an advance meeting about the Christmas ball."

"They're holding an emergency meeting because we're expecting a baby. Which makes you ineligible for the Christmas ball raffle. If you recall, Dante was the grand prize last Christmas. Your aunt had already determined that you were this year's sacrifice—I mean, prize. They'd planned advertising on barn roofs and everything, with slogans for you." River smiled. "Too bad you'll miss the fun."

"Not at all." Tighe was secretly relieved. "Who's the backup sacrifice?"

She shook her head. "I didn't ask."

"It's Galen's turn, if you ask me." He looked at Ash, who'd just walked into the kitchen. "You realize your turn at Fiona's chicanery will arrive one day. The bachelors will swarm this county."

His sister blanched. "I don't want to be swarmed. Don't talk about it."

"Don't worry. It'll be Galen or Jace on the griddle this year." Tighe looked at River. "Good to hear about the baby. I'll have Galen make you up a holistic protocol, if you'd like."

"Oh, you told him!" Ashlyn grinned at River, then Tighe. "Congratulations!" She threw her arms around his neck, giving him an octopus-like squeeze.

"Ash—" River began, and he gazed at her over his sister's shoulder.

"How does it feel to know you're going to be the father of triplets?" Ash asked, and Tighe watched River close her eyes as if she was in pain.

"Triplets?" He put Ash away from him gently.

River nodded, distinctly uncomfortable.

Joy swept Tighe fast, and amazement, and maybe even a little light-headedness, so that laughter burst from him. He couldn't stop laughing even if he'd tried.

"Whew," Ash said, "he's finally gone around the bend. One tap too many to the old brain stem."

River looked concerned. "Is he going to be all right?"

He wrapped her in his arms, kissing her on the forehead. "This is great! I win!"

His sister shook her head as if he were mentally slow. "This isn't Firefreak. You didn't just win a buckle. I'm pretty sure you haven't won anything—yet."

"Three kids—that's more than anybody else in the family. Just call me 'straight shooter' from now on." He laughed with delight. "If I was playing the one-armed bandit, I just hit Jackpot!"

River pushed him away. "Tighe, I have to get back to the gathering."

"We're going to visit later," he told her. "We have to talk this out, River."

She disappeared into the den. Ash looked at him. "I remember the days when you claimed you had her in the bag."

He did. Surely he did. He had to. "Are you part of Fiona's whiz-bang planning committee?"

"To give away my brothers? I wouldn't visit any of you on some poor unsuspecting female."

He shrugged. "So let's head out to find the chief."

River walked back into the kitchen and put teacups on the counter. "Oh, no, you don't. You're not leaving me here with the gang of matchmakers. I'm going, too."

Tighe blinked. "I don't think the babies should ride over rough terrain, do you?"

Ash took his arm, led him toward the door. "I think it's best if we head out before your feet get permanently stuck in your mouth, brother. Come on, River. We'll put him in the back."

RIVER WAS PLENTY annoyed with Tighe, but more than anything she was annoyed with herself. Triplets! She still hadn't gotten over the shock. The physician said if she was very careful, she might last until February or even March. That meant giving up her bodyguard position soon. The doctor wanted to take every precaution.

She looked at Tighe, who'd chosen to seat himself next to her where he could situate his leg most comfortably. He grinned at her from under the brim of his cowboy hat.

"It's awesome, babe."

"It is not awesome. I mean, it is, but you're not, so don't tweak me."

He laughed. "In a week or two, you'll be trying to drag me to the altar."

"I don't think so."

His navy eyes practically danced with pride. He was really impressed with himself. River sighed and looked away.

"I'm so amazed by you," Tighe said.

She turned to face him. "Why?"

"Because you're such a fertile goddess. I would never have suspected you'd be the Callahan woman to turn up a three-in-a-row."

He grinned again, the handsomest man she'd ever seen, and River wanted ever so badly to smack him. She went back to perusing the scenery as it rushed past. "Why are we checking on Running Bear, Ash?"

"Because we just thought we would." She was non-committal, which was typical Callahan, and meant she wasn't going to give the real reason for the drive to the canyons.

"Hey." Tighe gave River's arm a little squeeze. "I couldn't sleep after you visited last night. If that was your goal, you succeeded, gorgeous. I may not sleep for a week. And you know," he said, his eyes laughing and devilish, "you'd best not waste any time visiting me again with the old naked-under-the-robe trick. I want to remember how you look now, before you're big as a house."

"Whoa, Tighe," Ash said. "Careful where you step with those big feet of yours."

"Course, you'll be beautiful when you're enormous, too," Tighe said, and River glared at him. "But everyone knows the body changes forever once—"

Ash slammed on the brakes, and Tighe pitched forward. "Nice driving, Ash."

His sister hopped out of the jeep. "Just trying to help you out, brother dearest. Come on, River. Peg leg can follow us at his own slow pace. That way we won't have to listen to him."

"That will be a relief." River sent him an irritated glance and went off with his sister. Tighe grabbed his crutch and made his way out of the truck toward the stone circle, aware that his sister was trying to warn him that he wasn't scoring with River.

He really didn't know how to score. The woman had been distant toward him for so long—except the night he'd made his way into her bed—that he hardly knew how to woo her.

But she was having his children—and that was nothing short of glorious.

Chapter Five

By the time Tighe caught up with his sister and River, he found them facing Wolf at the stone circle. River glanced at Tighe, watching for his reaction.

"Didn't we just see you?" he asked his uncle. "Not any happier about this meeting than I was in town."

"Just checking on the chief. Is it a crime to check on one's father?" Wolf said.

Tighe gave his uncle a long, level look. Perhaps this was the source of his recent sense that all was not well. "If you've harmed him, you'll answer to me."

Wolf laughed. "You're not exactly standing on two legs right now, nephew."

"Don't worry about me." Tighe glanced about, searching for any indication that Running Bear had been there before Wolf's unannounced arrival. "Why are you hanging around so much suddenly, anyway?"

"Just making sure all is right at Rancho Diablo. That's what family does, isn't it? Sticks together?"

Ash squared her shoulders, jutted her chin. "You're not family. Turns out blood isn't always thicker than water."

"That hurts, niece." Wolf smiled at River. "Heard

you're expecting, young lady. I hope you'll accept my congratulations."

River didn't say anything, but it was all Tighe could do not to lose his temper, which was what Wolf wanted. "We don't need any congratulations."

"Oh," Wolf said. "Is she having your children?" He gave a short, terse laugh. "I thought Jace had spent more time with the bodyguard—"

"That's enough," Tighe stated, cutting in. "Move along, Uncle, before things get ugly. It's getting close, if you know what I mean."

Wolf's seven men appeared from out of nowhere. "Not too close," Wolf said. "Think the odds are on my side."

Tighe heard the whistling sound of an arrow flying before it split the ground, shaft up, right between Wolf's boots. His men backed up a pace, looking to him for direction.

"Seems we've overstayed our welcome," Wolf said. "Just remember, I'm keeping my eye on you. In the end, I'll get what I want."

"Which is what?" Tighe snapped.

"The land. The Diablos, the silver. All of it. Once again, the cartel will run this area." Wolf grinned, but his expression didn't have any warmth in it. "Don't think I won't sacrifice the lot of you for what I want."

Another arrow whistled, piercing the ground at the toe of Wolf's boot.

"We're well-trained, Uncle," Ash said. "We've trained all our lives for this. Running Bear's kept us on a path to survive whatever you've got."

Tighe's insides curled a bit as his blond-haired, gamine sister glanced at Wolf's small army, her hands on her hips.

"You don't have enough men to take us out," Ash said.

"That's right," River stated, and Tighe's heart dropped into his boots. "The Callahans have backup."

"You?" Wolf laughed. "You won't be doing much of anything in a couple of months. You'll be lying in bed, no use to anyone. Just a host for your parasites."

Tighe started forward, but a war cry shattered the air, stopping him. Astonishment crossed the faces of Wolf's men.

"Time to go, boys," Wolf said, and they trooped off to a black truck with a double cab. Two men rode in the back, their guns pointing at the Callahans, covering their departure.

Tighe wanted to put his arms around River, but he could tell by the outraged expression on her face that all men were probably unwelcome in her space at the moment.

"That goon insulted me," she said, disgusted. "How dare he?"

"Pay no mind to Uncle Wolf," Ash soothed. "He's all sound and fury."

River looked at Tighe. "It was all I could do not to shoot him."

"I know. I could feel you quivering. I'm glad you didn't," Tighe said. "He's really not worth it."

"He doesn't like you. I'm going to have to keep an eye on you while you're incapacitated."

Tighe grinned. "Oh, darn."

"You can laugh," she said, "but as we know, you don't always make the best decisions. Witness your jaunt on Firefreak."

He felt his jaw drop. "That was the best decision I ever made!"

Ash laughed. "Come on. Let's go dig Grandfather

out of the shadows and find out how he wants us to proceed."

"I'm serious," River said. "You can't fire a gun while you're balancing on one good leg, Tighe."

He frowned. "I can shoot a needle off a cactus. You just start thinking about the rest of his conversation. That's the more immediate problem."

"Which is what?" River glared at him.

"You're going to be bed-bound soon," he pointed out, and Ash said, "Incoming. Lightning strike for brother with unfortunate mouth problem."

"And while we're on the subject of your pregnancy," Tighe said, feeling very righteous at the moment, "I don't want anybody thinking Jace is the father of your children. We're going to have to get married immediately."

"Why do I have the dumbest brothers on the planet?" Ash moaned.

The trio made their way to a rock ledge, heading toward where the last arrow had originated. It was hard to tell where they might find the chief, since the arrows had come from opposite directions.

"Your uncle was just trying to get your goat," River said. "He succeeded. But that doesn't mean I'm going to do anything about it."

"The boys will want their parents to be married," Tighe pointed out, doing his best to think of any reason to convince the beautiful woman at his side to think of him in a romantic light.

"Grandfather!" Ash exclaimed. "Am I glad to see you! Break these two up, will you?"

Running Bear smiled. "They are meant to be together. Hello, Tighe. River." He looked at his grandson. "Now you understand the path of your spirit."

"Do I?" Tighe frowned. "She won't cooperate."

"No, I won't." River matched his frown. "And the only reason I'm having your children is because you wouldn't cooperate with what your family wanted!"

"A marriage ceremony can be performed now," Running Bear said with a pleased smile.

River sent Tighe a startled look. "Now? As in, right here?"

"I get to be the maid of honor!" Ash exclaimed.

"Now, wait a minute," River began, and Tighe took her hand in his.

"Thank you, Grandfather. It would be an honor if you would join us," Tighe said.

"Hang on," River said. "First, I never said I would marry you. And you haven't asked."

"I did," Tighe said. "You just said no."

Running Bear and Ash laughed.

"She's a good match for you," the chief stated.

"I know, Grandfather." He considered the bodyguard with the whiskey-colored hair and the lifted brow challenging him. "She's strong."

"And don't forget it," River said. "When I finally do have to stay in bed, I don't want to hear one word about my delicate state or weakened condition. I'm a bodyguard, and I always will be."

"I know. Will you say yes now?" Tighe asked, hoping against hope that River would accept him. She could be stubborn, more so even than Ashlyn or Fiona, and that was saying something. His sons would inherit a huge stubborn streak! It would work well for them.

"No, thank you," River said. "I'm sorry, but I hate

being rushed. And I'm not happy about your uncle and what he said. I don't like to make big decisions when I'm not happy." She looked at Running Bear. "Thank you for the offer, though, Chief. It would be a great honor to have you bless our marriage. But your grandson is too wild-eyed for me. We don't know each other very well. I hope you can understand, Chief." She went back down the trail the way they'd come.

"Shot down," Ash said with a sigh. "I'm so sorry, brother. On the other hand, I'm not really surprised. That Jace business annoyed her, but she has spent more time with him over the past year. She and Ana both. Of course, we know they just see him as an irritating kid brother, but…" Ash shook her head, sending him a sorrowful look. "Even Storm Cash's lady friend, Lulu Feinstrom, asked me if Jace and River were an item when I was in town today. So you see why Wolf easily found your underbelly on that one."

Tighe sighed. "It's all right. Well, it's not all right, but it will be soon. I hope." He'd work on River a little more, try to get her to see that he adored her from her toes to her nose, and then, maybe, she'd realize she just simply couldn't live without him.

He certainly couldn't live without her.

In the upstairs library where the private Callahan meetings were held, Tighe didn't fare much better than he had with River. His brothers and sister gazed at him with sympathy, approbation and some disappointment.

"We need every one of us to be clear-eyed and clear-minded," Galen said. "No more risky behavior."

The gazes landed on Tighe again.

He didn't say anything for a minute, but when it

became clear that his siblings expected to extract a promise of better behavior from him, he sighed. "My leg will be fine in a week or so. Then I'll be right back to my old, lethal self."

"Good." Galen nodded. "Jace, until then, you stick close to the women."

"No," Tighe said. "He can manage every other woman on the ranch. I'll handle River."

"No one's managing or handling anyone," Ash said. "Galen wants one guard near the houses, and one on Fiona and Burke. He wants the canyons staked out, and the outlying bunkhouse, and so on. Don't make this difficult, Tighe."

There'd been enough gossip about Jace and River. Tighe aimed to set folks straight on that really quick— just as soon as he could figure out how to get his elusive girlfriend to an altar. Girlfriend? He pondered his brandy. Would River call herself his girlfriend?

He doubted it. "River's having my children, so it makes sense for me to stay close to her."

"I wouldn't put it exactly that way to her," Ash reminded him. "River thinks she's looking out for you, and I can't argue with her, considering your physical condition."

"There's nothing wrong with my— Never mind." He was darn tired of everyone reminding him that he was the weak link. "You guys can keep ribbing me about Firefreak, but I'm telling you, riding him was the moment I found my destiny. Just like Dante." He glared at his twin.

Dante shook his head. "I didn't find my destiny on the back of a stupid hunk of meat. I found my destiny in Ana's bed."

His brothers all whistled, and Ash looked disgusted.

"I hope whoever I end up with doesn't talk about me the way you meatheads talk about the women in your lives."

"I'll chat with Xav Phillips about it. Let him know you don't go for possessive, alpha males." Galen ruffled his sister's hair, and she spared him an aggrieved glance. "Back to business. It probably would be best if you stayed here at the ranch, Tighe. You're not much use at the fence or in the canyons, since you can't ride a horse. So you'll stay with the women and children."

"Oh, for the love of Mike," he grumbled. "Leave me a shred of dignity?"

"Jace, you ride fence. Ash, you stick with Fiona." Galen looked at Sloan and Falcon. "I'll cover the outlying bunkhouse and talk to the foremen." He glanced around the room. "Does anybody have anything they want to bring up?"

"Yeah," Tighe said. "As soon as I'm able, I'm planning to ride Firefreak again."

They all stared at him.

Ash smacked her forehead with her palm. "Next time, I hope you land on your head!"

"If you hadn't sent River to my room to keep me from riding—" he reminded his siblings, and they all booed him down.

"I'm going to be a father now, and my lady won't marry me. It's because I didn't finish exploring my calling. I'm playing matters too risk averse."

"Nope. It's because of the wish I made of the universe," Dante said with glee. "It's going to happen to Jace, and Galen, too. To all of you, because you all made my life such a living heck on my way to true love."

"What wish?" his siblings demanded.

"I wished you all would fall for partners who understand the thrill of the chase, and would give you a good long slippery run, where there's lots of crow to be eaten at every bend in the road." Dante looked pleased with himself. "I said it into the wind, and the words took life. Obviously."

"That's terrible," Ash said. "How could you?"

"I don't believe in that kind of nonsense," Tighe said. "My problem has nothing to do with you. River is superindependent, and she thinks our one night together was a mistake. A setup."

Ash sighed. "This is all my fault."

Tighe nodded, glad to see someone taking responsibility for his situation. "You didn't stop me from riding."

"No, I didn't, but not for lack of trying. I hope you'll be a better father than you are a bull rider," she said. "I hope you have three darling little girls to run you ragged. It would be your just deserts."

His mouth turned down. "I'm having three boys. I'm positive that's what I'll have. I like the color blue, and I like boy sports. I don't think I could handle three Fiona-type youth-size blessings in my life." He gazed at his sister, taking in his petite firecracker of a sibling. "Or a female like you, for that matter."

Galen stood. "Let's get back to our ranch issues. Running Bear is worried about the fact that Wolf has practically made himself at home on our land."

"Home is where the heart is," Tighe muttered. "Wolf's heart isn't here. He's just greedy. And I believe scared."

"Scared?" Jace demanded. "How do you figure that?"

"I think the cartel's hanging something over him. My gut tells me he cut a deal with them and now he needs to deliver. The fact that Wolf's followed this thing for so long makes me think either the payoff is huge or he made too large of a promise to the cartel and now they're forcing him to ramp up his activity here—or both."

"Either way, it's not good," Sloan said.

"No. I keep trying to figure his next move, but he always surprises me," Ash said.

"What are we going to do about Storm?" Tighe asked. "Sloan, you honestly feel good about having Storm's niece, Sawyer, guarding your twins?"

Sloan shrugged. "River keeps a pretty tight eye on Sawyer, if you haven't noticed."

He hadn't, probably because he was too busy trying to keep a tight eye on River without looking like an overpossessive, sex-hungry doof. "River's not going to be able to do that for long. She'll be housebound before she wants to be." There was no question River wouldn't be the kind of woman who enjoyed sitting in her bed watching TV and reading books, even for a few months. Or a few hours.

She'd probably think it was the nearest thing to incarceration. No doubt she wouldn't look on him any more kindly than she did now, once she hadn't seen sunlight and ridden a horse in the fresh air for a couple of months.

"Earth to Tighe," Ash said. "Are you listening?"

"Probably not too well," Galen said. "Does he ever?"

"It's true," Tighe agreed. "I don't always have the best auditory skills."

"Selective hearing is what ails you, bro," Jace said.

"Maybe. The key is to say something important. That's the way to command my attention," he said helpfully.

Ash sighed. "Let's adjourn this meeting. We're all strung too tightly to make much headway."

"I'm not strung tightly. I feel just fine." Tighe got up, limped to the door. "But I don't have a problem with adjourning."

"Because you want to go find River," Ash said.

"True. Seems like something a wise man would do at this moment." He thought about the beautiful body-guard and wished he knew how to romance her bet-ter. "Just can't figure out where I'm going wrong with that little lady."

His brothers and sister gathered around him, thump-ing him on the back. They stared out the windows of the upstairs library, gazing out over the ranch.

"Listen!" Tighe said suddenly, his ears on alert. It was unmistakable, the sound of hooves pounding, rush-ing along rock trails that time had cut into the canyons. "The Diablos."

The Callahans glanced at each other, standing to-gether united. The mystical Diablos were a portent of things to come, according to legend. Tighe's scalp prickled. There had already been so much change— but he'd felt the signs in the wind, too. He'd known something was coming.

Running Bear had warned of impending darkness. He'd warned of a hunted one. Was the warning com-ing to pass now?

If it's me, I'll go off and live in the canyons where no one can find me. I'll never hurt this family in any way. I was brought here to save it.

Ash leaned her head against him. "Whatever it is, we stand together."

He nodded, and their brothers murmured their agreement.

The bond was unbreakable.

Chapter Six

Tighe was pretty shocked when his bedroom door creaked open, the sound somehow loud in the still bunkhouse. He didn't move while the intruder crept slowly, deliberately toward his bed. Tighe's gun was under his pillow, and the element of surprise would be on his side. By his military watch, he could see the time was 2200 hours. Late. So he waited, holding his breath, coiled like a spring.

His nocturnal visitor bumped the bed, and still Tighe didn't move.

The sheet and blanket lifted, and a warm body slid in next to him.

"Hello?" he said, just as River's sexy form melded against his side.

"Hi. Do you mind?"

"Not at all." His brain raced with relief and the good fortune that something had brought her to his bed. "What's going on?"

"I want to talk to you. This is the best place to do it. No prying eyes and listening ears."

So much curvy softness pressed up against him it was smoking his synapses. It was hard to think about conversation when her perfume teased at him. "Sawyer watching the twins?"

"They're with Sloan and Kendall. I think Sawyer went to see her uncle. I'm off duty, Kendall says, because she wants me to rest." River sighed. "I don't want everyone babying me just because I'm carrying triplets."

He hadn't expected her to feel any differently. "So what can I do for you?"

"Fiona wants me to try on the magic wedding dress. She says I'm running out of time if I want to know the truth."

He frowned in the dark. "Truth about what?"

"Whether we belong together."

"Listen, you know you belong to me, because we're having three babies. It has nothing to do with Fiona's myths."

"Ana says it's not a myth."

He sighed. "Trust me, I've heard this tale over and over again. I'm a big believer in spirits and angels and things that guide us. Probably no bigger believer in the family than me. Tell me a story about things that go bump in the night, and I'm all over it. But a magic dress is too much for me."

"I thought you'd feel that way. So I told her I'd try it on if you didn't object."

He sat up to lean against the rustic wood headboard. "Anything that gets you to thinking about a wedding is worth encouraging. So now that I'm wide-awake and thinking about it, I vote yes on trying on the infamous gown. I've got a fifty-fifty chance it goes my way, right? Either I'm Prince Charming or I'm not. I'm feeling good about it." He smiled, pleased with himself. If there was truth to the gown's fantastical leanings, then it would definitely reveal him to be River's one true love. She was having his triplets, and nothing could deny that. There wasn't a charm on the planet that could take away the fact that he and River were together forever.

Maybe she'd fall so in love with the gown she'd be anxious to head straight to the altar. The sooner the better. There was a time constraint issue here. Tighe knew River pretty well, and figured if he wagered on her being the kind of woman who wouldn't get married once the three little boys added their sweetness to her already sweet figure, it was a wager he'd win. "The more I think about it, the more I believe you ought to listen to Aunt Fiona."

"Why do I have the feeling that your initial reaction was your gut, and true, reaction? Even though I can't see your face, you're not that hard to read, Tighe."

"I'm an open book," he said cheerfully. "Is that all you came to visit me about? Get my permission to try on the family gown?"

"I don't need your permission."

"So go for it. I don't hold much stock in it, but the other Callahan ladies swear by it. Although they never share their experience, so all I know is that the gown seems to be a good luck talisman of some kind, since all my brothers end up at the altar. Including Dante, which was a miracle, in my mind." Tighe tucked his arm around her, pulled her up against him, but she wriggled away. He felt her leave the bed. "Hey, where are you going?"

"Back to my room."

"I enjoyed you flashing me the other night. I wouldn't mind a repeat performance, beautiful."

That didn't win him anything but a raised brow, so he shifted gears as fast as he could. "Stay awhile longer. I've got some things on my mind, too."

She slid back in, but he could feel her tension, so didn't try to wrap her against him again. "I want to go with you to your next doctor's appointment. If you wouldn't mind."

"That's fine."

Easy. Almost too easy. Tighe decided to press his advantage. "I'm hoping you'll let me give my children my name."

"You mean if we don't get married."

"Right. Does seem the right thing to do." He was asking as nicely as he knew how without downright putting his foot down.

"I think that would be best. Thank you."

Great. All hurdles cleared—except the big one. But now wasn't the time to press her about marriage. He'd have to be satisfied with tiny steps.

"Tighe, I don't want you riding bulls anymore. Including Firefreak."

He blinked in the darkness, surprised. "Why not?"

"Because you're apparently not that... I mean, I'm going to need help with the children, after they're born. You'll have healed in the next several months, before I give birth. After that it will probably be as exciting around here as riding bulls."

"You're right. I agree."

He felt her turn her face toward him, longed to put his arms around her and kiss her thoroughly.

"So you'll stay away from the rodeo?"

"If you'll stay out of the canyons and close to the house, where one of my brothers—or preferably me—will be with you at all times."

"That won't be a problem," River said, "if you put a recliner near a window for me. I don't think I can bear to be in a bed for a month without looking out the window."

"I'll buy you a top of the line, brand-new recliner. You'll feel like a queen."

She slid out of the bed. He didn't ask her to remain—he knew she wouldn't. But at least she'd come to see him, felt comfortable getting into his bed.

"Good night, Tighe."

The words flew out of his mouth before he could stop them. "Make love with me."

He felt her hesitation.

"How?"

"Well, first, you get back in my bed," Tighe said, "and then I'm going to kiss you. Then I'll probably slide your clothes off one by one, with my teeth, no doubt, just because it sounds like fun and we didn't do that last time. And then—"

"I meant," River said, interrupting his wistful soliloquizing, "if we're not getting married, how could we make love? Why would we repeat what got us into this mess?"

"Details, details." Reaching out, he pulled her back into his bed. "We don't have to make love tonight. Let's just sleep together. Get to know each other better. It's hard to get to know someone very well unless I'm in a bed with them."

"I'll bet," River said, and he laughed.

"You're going to be such a feisty little mother."

She sighed, but he noticed she didn't wriggle out of his arms. "I'll try not to let the females of this family down."

"That's right. Tradition is very important to us." She felt so good he could barely stand to keep his hands to himself. "Any chance you're cold? Need a tall, dark, handsome blanket to warm you up and maybe make you the happiest woman on earth?"

She giggled. "You don't think much of yourself, do you?"

He snuggled into her neck, smelled the flowery scent of her hair. "I believe I recall it was all you could do not to yell down Ms. Sherby's B and B, beautiful."

River pinched him. "You were the only one making noise, cowboy."

This was true, as he recalled. Making love to River—finally, after months and months of dry-mouthed mooning—had been a dizzying, crazy ride. "Let me relive that moment. I promise not to yell this time."

"Personally, I think you'll always be noisy, Tighe. Because of your reputation for being silent, you've repressed a lot of sound."

He kissed her cheek, inched a hand across her stomach, slowly making his move. "Let's find out."

"You just want to make love to me before I get big as a house."

"Indeed. And then, too." He kissed her neck, stole across to her lips. "I promise that no matter how large you become, I'll always be able to handle it."

"You're about to get yourself in big trouble, cowboy," River said. But he noticed she wasn't pushing him away, so he decided kissing her needed to be done at once.

She opened up to him like a sweet flower. A groan escaped him, and she giggled.

"You see? You're the noisy one."

He slid a hand up, captured a breast. "Give me a

couple hours. If I don't yell, you can come back tomorrow night. How's that for a deal?"

"We'll see," River said.

AFTER THE NIGHT River spent in Tighe's arms, she knew she had to take the path the other Callahan women had journeyed.

There was no reason to wait. Either she and Tighe were a one-night fling that had resulted in children, and therefore she'd had no business being in his bed last night—or they were meant to be together. Either way, there was no time to lose. It felt as if her waistline had already put on a couple inches—though when she measured, it was more like one. Tighe hadn't seemed to notice, although she did think he'd been much more careful—less wild sexually—than the previous time they'd made love.

She didn't believe the treasured family gown would tell her whether Tighe was her man, but she did wonder if putting the silly thing on would make her feel more as if becoming a bride was the right thing to do. That bothered her most of all—the itching, nagging feeling that maybe marrying in haste would mean a lifetime of regrets.

Her parents had been divorced. She was going to try to avoid that uneasy route.

"Hello, River," Fiona trilled. "You're up bright and early, aren't you? Shouldn't you be resting?"

She had a feeling Fiona would be tickled if she learned River probably hadn't had two hours of sleep last night, thanks to Tighe. "Fiona, you offered to let me try on the magic wedding dress, and—"

"Oh, my dear!" The older woman beamed. "Are you warming up to my wonderful nephew?"

"Perhaps. Slowly," River admitted, not wanting to put Fiona into full-tilt wedding machinations.

"Slowly is fine. Can't rush a good thing. The best things in life are worth waiting for and all that." She pointed with her spatula to the stairs. "You just go on up into the attic, close the door so you'll have privacy and try it on. I'd show you where it is, but I'm deep into making waffles for the crew." She smiled again. "I'm so happy you've decided to give the dress a try."

"Thank you." River went up to the attic, amazed that anxiety set in as she ascended the stairs. Her steps slowed as she entered the enormous room made homey by window seats and a dangling chandelier. It was only a dress, and a myth. A legend that made the Callahans happy.

Ana had had a bit of a rocky time with the dress, although River didn't know the particulars. She just knew the dress wasn't a panacea, a magic wand, for her relationship with Tighe.

When he made love to her, it was hard for her to think there was anything wrong with their relationship—which was the problem. It was all about sex, and a purely sexual relationship didn't last.

Although she could easily imagine wanting to make love to Tighe for the rest of her life.

She glanced around the room, noting a cheval mirror, a couple of small chairs and tables, a cozy nook in which one could read—or plot, in Fiona's case. River opened the door to the long closet, easily locating the bag that contained the gown. It was the only item hanging in the cavernous walk-in space.

She took the bag—it was surprisingly light for holding a fabulous, magical wedding dress—hung it on a hook near the cheval mirror and with sudden excitement, gently drew the zipper down.

Chapter Seven

Tighe hurried into the kitchen, spotting his aunt Fiona with relief. Maybe there was still time to stop River from trying on the magic wedding dress.

"Hello, favored nephew. How about some waffles?" Fiona asked. "And maybe some eggs?"

"No, thanks, Aunt Fiona." He glanced around quickly. "Has River been here?"

"A little bit ago. But she's not here now. Bacon?"

"It looks great, but I'm kind of in a hurry. Did she say where she was going?"

"She did," Fiona said, "but I don't know if I'm to divulge her location."

He glanced up at the ceiling toward the attic. "She's up there, isn't she? I'm too late."

"For what?" Fiona gave him a curious look.

"To stop her."

"Gracious me, why would you want to?" Fiona shook her head, her eyes rounded. "I thought you were all hot to get River to the altar."

"I am. But Dante just told me that the dress backfired on him in rare fashion.

"Oh, pooh. Don't listen to your twin." Fiona laid a plate in front of Tighe to tempt him. "You and Dante may be from the same zygote, but truthfully, you're total opposites."

"This is serious, Aunt. Dante said it was months before he saw Ana again after she tried on the gown. He said it messed everything up for him." Tighe felt very desperate on this score. "I've got enough trouble on my hands with River without that kind of supernatural assistance." He'd just sweet-talked her into his bed, and the pleasure had been mind-bending. He wanted more of that! Intimacy was the way to get his woman to the altar, not a gown. "Trust me, I've got this covered."

"I believe that's what you said about Firefreak, and about River," Fiona observed. "I do believe you could do with a little help in some matters, nephew."

His gaze fastened on the ceiling. "I don't suppose there's any way to stop her?"

"You could," Fiona said, "but I wouldn't recommend seeing her in the gown. If you go charging up there, that's what might happen. And I don't know how that would affect matters." She shook her head. "Every woman has had her time alone with the gown. Her time to figure out what she really wants."

"Damn it." He sank onto a bar stool, contemplated the delicious eggs, waffle and bacon without enthusiasm.

"Oh, no! Whatever you do, don't curse the gown," Fiona warned.

"I'm not. I'm cursing myself. I'm sort of cursing why I didn't just keep her in bed with me this morning. I could have told her my leg was acting up. I could have told her—"

"Pardon me," Fiona said, her face wreathed with sudden delight, "not to be indelicate, but you did just let something slip."

"Sorry," he muttered. "I didn't mean to be unchivalrous. I do apologize, Aunt."

Fiona cleared her throat. "However, all that being said, you and River have something of a rapprochement, then?"

"All I can tell you is that I'm gaga for her, and I'm real nervous about her being in your attic of drama."

Fiona patted his hand. "Everything will work out."

He couldn't stand it. Dante had scared the heck out of him. Tighe didn't want to be separated from River for months. He had enough problems—why had he endorsed Fiona's magic bag of tricks?

Still, a man couldn't deny his lady a chance to try on a beautiful gown, could he?

"I'm scared. I've never been scared like this before."

"Nephew!" Fiona ladled more food onto his plate, though he hadn't touched a bite. "I've never seen you like this! For a man with a huge adventurous streak, you're a nervous wreck!"

He slid off the stool, went to the stairwell. "It's too quiet up there. I'm going up."

"I really cannot counsel you to do so," Fiona said, worried. She came to stand at his side. "Just call up there, if you're so concerned, but I won't vouch for what happens. I'm pretty sure it's a man-free zone. And I don't know if River will appreciate you being a Nervous Nelly."

Maybe he overestimated the gown's importance. But what if he had the same misfortune Dante had suffered? Tighe had just lured River back into his arms! He wasn't letting go of her again, not after he'd waited like a dying man for her to soften toward him.

Making love to her was the sweetest thing he'd ever experienced in his life and there hadn't been a whole lot of sweetness in his twenty-eight years. He'd waited a very long time for River to even look his way. Dante and he had waited a long time for the nanny bodyguards to do more than say hello—and the night Tighe had caught River and his siblings plotting to keep him off Firefreak, he'd felt no compunction whatsoever about turning the tables on her and seducing her.

Only the tables had been turned on him big-time— and he'd tumbled like a rock into a pond. Now he'd been given a second chance, and that second chance had been ever so delicious and tantalizing last night.

He just couldn't risk it.

He charged up the stairs.

RIVER SAT IN one of the window seats, staring out the window, thinking. She'd put the dress bag away, closed the closet door.

It had been the most amazing thing. Yet somehow unsettling. Very unsettling.

She'd try again in a moment. Try to work up her courage to do it. She had drawn the zipper down, and just as quickly, zipped the bag back up.

She heard boots thundering on the stairs and jumped when Tighe burst into the attic. "Tighe!"

He came to a dead halt. Gave her a funny look when he spotted her sitting in the window seat. "Am I too late?"

"Too late for what?"

"To stop you from trying on the dress."

Her brows rose. "Why would you want to?"

He seemed upset, which confused her. "I just had a funny feeling you shouldn't. It was like something came over the wires, if you know what I mean, that told me this wasn't an idea that was going to go in our favor."

"You told me to go for it."

"I know," Tighe admitted, "but like I said, it was like I received some kind of weird message from the ozone."

"It doesn't entirely surprise me that you'd receive a weird message," River said with a sigh, "because sometimes you do seem a bit weird. Like the other Callahans, at times." Still, he did seem bothered about something. "Anyway, I didn't try it on. I never even looked at it."

"Why not?"

She shrugged. "Maybe I got the same message you did."

He seemed relieved. "That's a good sign, if we're getting the same thoughts."

"Maybe. I wouldn't put money on it." She looked at Tighe. "I've decided to throw caution to the wind and marry you regardless of what the magic wedding dress might have to say."

"Really?" He was obviously surprised.

"Yeah." River went to turn off the lamp. "Marriage isn't a decision to be made by a magic eight ball. I don't want a gown to tell me what to do—even if I did believe in such things."

"You're going to marry me?"

She sighed. "Yes, Tighe. But it's a practical decision, not a romantic thing."

"I don't think so," he said. "I don't think we were being practical last night when we made love. In fact, I'm pretty sure we were being romantic. At least I was. And I intend to be even more romantic, especially because in a couple of months, you're not going to care about romancing."

She glared at him. "I don't know what you mean about last night."

"What I mean is that the earth moved for both of us last night. And I was not silent. Neither were you. Birds flew out of trees. Critters ran from the ranch. You, my love, express your pleasure loudly enough that we're going to have to move into the bunkhouse near the canyons, and even then, I'll have to sound-proof the house."

She felt a blush steal up her cheeks. "You're embarrassing me."

"Don't be," he said cheerfully. "I liked it."

She walked to the top of the stairs. "It's a practical matter, Tighe. We're having children. It would be best for them if we married. I'm not repeating last night."

He stepped over to her, took her in his arms, closed the attic door. Kissed her long and hard, then his kisses turned gentle. River felt her knees weaken. Her fingers stole into his hair, then gripped his shoulders. He made short work of her skirt, murmured something about "magic wedding dresses being no help," then sat down and moved her into his lap. She grabbed the zipper on his jeans, and faster than she'd undone the dress bag, had his zipper down, gasping when he entered her. She tried to cover her moans of pleasure by burying her face in his neck while he dug his hands into her buttocks, pulling her tighter against him.

Glorious heat exploded all through her, and she couldn't help moving, rocking, hard against him. Tighe groaned, held her tight and still, and collapsed against her, the two of them gasping with pleasure.

"No more talk of practicality," he said after a moment. "I can't stay away from you long enough to be practical."

"All right," River gasped. She felt so bone-meltingly lovely she would have agreed to just about anything at this moment. "But it's not romance, either."

"Not everything is a business decision," Tighe said, cradling her against his chest, supporting her weight as he relaxed against the window seat. "You just let me make you happy like this every day, and we'll worry about what to call it later."

He wasn't listening. Their relationship wasn't romantic. It was sex.

Yet it wasn't just sex. She'd been crazy about this cowboy forever. "Whatever you say," she finally murmured, too satisfied to argue.

"That's my girl," he said, and River giggled.

"You're going to get in trouble with me, cowboy. Chauvinism is not romantic nor practical."

"I'll work on it."

"You do that." She fell silent, feeling slightly guilty. She hadn't been totally honest—not honest at all. She had unzipped the bag. She *had* looked at the gown.

But when she'd pulled it from its covering, it had turned black. Black as the ace of spades. And turned into tactical gear, something to be worn in a war zone, or at least a very dangerous place.

Frightened, she'd stuffed it back in the bag and rudely shoved it into the closet.

She wasn't going to tell a soul. But even she knew that a magic wedding dress that turned black was a bad omen. Chills ran over her skin.

"Cold?" Tighe asked.

"A little," she said. "Let's go downstairs."

They moved slowly away from each other, rearranged their clothes. She could hardly look at him, even when he touched her chin, held her close to him. Kissed her, long and sweet. "I'll talk to Grandfather. We can marry this weekend."

"Fine," River said, and went to the door.

No enchanted gown was going to cost her the chance to marry the father of her children, the cowboy of her dreams. Maybe he'd regret their marriage later—after all, the gown was a Callahan gown and probably was fine-tuned to Callahan emotion—but after worrying and wondering over what she should do, River decided to catch her cowboy.

Making love with Tighe had convinced her.

She wasn't about to give him up, even if she had to battle a disapproving magic wedding dress to do it.

TIGHE FELT AS IF the world had just smiled on him. Everything was going better than he'd hoped at this stage in the game.

This was awesome.

"Let me take you downstairs. Fiona's made breakfast," he said, leading River out of the attic. "I'm sure my little boys would love a waffle right about now."

"No one has said we're having boys."

He loved teasing her. She probably wanted three little girls. He didn't care, as long as he was getting three of everything she wanted to give him. How many men could say that a woman gave him three babies?

He stopped on the stairs. "Do you hear that?"

She stopped beside him. "I don't hear anything."

"Exactly. And something's burning."

She grabbed his arm. "It's the food!"

He practically broad-jumped the rest of the stairs to hurry into the kitchen. "Find my aunt," he said. "I'll put this fire out." Bacon grease smoked in the frying pan, the bacon black. Eggs lay cold to the side, and the waffle iron held a blackened waffle. He shut that off, too, glancing over his shoulder as River hurried back into the kitchen.

"I can't find her," she told him.

A horrible feeling crept over him, spreading like spilled ink. Grabbing his phone, he texted an alert to his siblings. *Think we've got trouble. Can't find Fiona.*

It didn't take long for the back door to blow open. Jace and Galen came charging in. They looked at the ruined food, saw River trying to air the smoke out of the kitchen.

"This is not good," Galen said. "I've never known Fiona to burn anything."

"No kidding." That was the understatement of the year.

"She can't just disappear," Jace said as the door flew open again and Ash hurried in.

"What's happened?" She looked at River. "Weren't you here with her?"

"I was upstairs," River said.

"And you didn't hear anything?" Ash demanded. "Didn't smell the kitchen practically burning down?"

River gave Tighe a startled look, and he said, "Easy, Ash. Neither one of us noticed anything out of the ordinary. Fiona was her usual cheerful self when I walked through, and I was the last to see her."

Sloan and Dante hurried through the den into the kitchen. "She can't have gotten far," Sloan said. "Someone have Falcon start tracking her."

"I'll do it," Jace said. "I'm the best tracker in the family."

"Not better than me," Ash said, pushing past him.

"You two stick together," Tighe said.

"Got it," Ash called back.

"Okay, fan out. River, you stay here, in case she comes back," Tighe began, but she scowled at him.

"I'm a bodyguard, Tighe."

"And pregnant," he said. "Stay here, please. Just in case she returns."

"Who's going to watch *her*?" Galen asked, tipping his chin toward River. "If something has happened to Fiona—"

"Where's Burke?" River suddenly asked. "I checked their room, but he's not there."

"I just saw him out in the corral," Sloan said. "I'll go tell him." He trudged off, not eager to relay bad news.

The brothers divided up the rest of Rancho Diablo to search for tracks, and they all took off. "I'll be right back," Tighe told River, who favored him with another scowl. "I'm sorry. You can't ride with us. It's dangerous, and this isn't your fight. Be home base for us, and let us know if Fiona shows up here. All right?"

River nodded. He brushed a swift kiss against her lips, and she threw her arms around him. "Find her, Tighe."

"We will."

"Do you want me to call Sheriff Cartwright? Just in case she's been in town for some reason?"

Fiona wouldn't have left a mess. Yet Wolf had been frequenting town more and more. "It's a great idea. Thanks."

Tighe kissed her one final time and headed out.

Chapter Eight

By nightfall, everyone in the town of Diablo and the surrounding county knew Fiona Callahan was missing. They also knew she hadn't simply wandered off—the sheriff and his deputies had pointed out signs of struggle in the dirt outside. Running Bear had come by, gravely examining the scene in the kitchen, then standing quietly for a long time, his eyes closed. River hadn't known what to say—she'd felt guilty every time the sheriff or his deputies had asked her if she'd heard anything strange.

She hadn't noticed a thing. Lost in her daydreams of Tighe, she'd been focused on the gown, and him. Not doing her job of guarding the Callahans.

Worse, she'd left the twins with Sawyer Cash—and no matter what Kendall said, River couldn't help wondering if Sawyer might have signaled to her uncle Storm or someone that no one was on duty except her, making it the perfect time to strike.

If the Callahans weren't worried about Sawyer, why should she be? Anyway, it seemed as if Jace was keeping a fairly close eye on Sawyer.

River sank onto a bar stool in the kitchen, considered the counters she'd scrubbed until they shone. After the sheriff and deputies and Running Bear left, she'd cleaned the room, throwing out the ruined food and mopping the floor. It was still a pretty sad space without Fiona's cheerful mess in it.

Ana walked into the kitchen and plunked down next to her. "You should be sitting in the den, relaxing on that nice comfy leather sofa."

"I can't relax. I'm so worried." She looked at Ana. "I feel terrible that Fiona needed me and I was up in the attic." She closed her eyes for a moment. *Being utterly, wonderfully seduced.*

"Don't fixate on that. Whoever grabbed her had been watching the house, saw an opening. Everybody here is some kind of operative or bodyguard, and still, they managed to grab the one of us nobody expected would ever be under threat. Fiona isn't exactly new to this rodeo. She knows how to be careful." Ana hugged River. "There's nothing you could have done."

"Except be in the kitchen with her. Where I should have been, and not in the attic."

"All of us visit the attic on occasion. And the basement, to find the holiday lights and Fiona's delicious preserves. Basement, attic, makes no difference. We had our guard down, and someone noticed. We can't beat ourselves up about it." Ana sighed. "It will all work out, anyway. The Callahans aren't going to let anything happen to their aunt."

"I feel horrible for Burke. He looked like he aged five years when they told him she was gone." River felt as if she might cry, forced the tears back. "He's in his room right now. The sheriff told him to stay put. I think he's afraid Burke might have a heart attack from the stress."

"I'll check on him in a minute." Ana looked at her

best friend. "Come on. I insist you lie down on the sofa."

"I can't." Still, she followed Ana into the other room, glad to get away from the kitchen, which was depressing without Fiona. "Wait. You're here to guard me, aren't you? Did Tighe send you?"

"Yes, and yes. And don't argue. Lie down." Ana forced her to do so, then tossed a soft afghan over her even though it was hot as blazes outside.

They didn't speak for a long time. Ana probably hoped she'd fall asleep, but River couldn't, not while Fiona was in danger. Too many worried thoughts ran through her head. She tried not to think about the what-ifs, but it was hard.

"So, triplets," Ana said. "That'll put Tighe in the race for the ranch." She laughed, shaking her head. "Not that any of us believe there is such a thing. But Fiona will do anything to see her nephews happily married."

If Fiona came back. River could hardly bear to think of it. "Did you ever imagine when we came to work here that we'd end up married to two of the brothers?"

Ana shook her head. "Kind of nice, though."

River got up from the sofa, paced to the window. "I wish we'd hear something."

"Me, too."

"You left Sawyer with the twins?"

"Kendall's got them. She wanted to come over and keep you company, but Sloan said no. He's too worried, since Fiona was kidnapped from here. Unless she wandered off..."

The comment hung in the air. They both knew Fiona wouldn't have wandered off. Her mind was fully clear, and never more clear than when she was cooking for her nephews. "She didn't. She had fresh dough for waffles, and eggs sitting out."

Ana came to stand beside River. "Worrying won't help, and it's not good for the triplets."

"I know."

"Ever since Tighe found out you're expecting, he's been a different man." Ana laughed. "These Callahans insist they'll always be single, until they find out they're going to be a father."

"Don't remind me." She wanted to believe Tighe would romance her this way even if she wasn't pregnant with his children.

He wouldn't.

Running Bear walked into the den, and River saw pain on his face. "How are you doing, Chief?"

He looked drawn. "I know where they took her."

River gasped. "Where?"

"They took Fiona to their hideout in Montana. Same place they took Taylor."

"Oh, no!" River looked at Ana. "But why?"

"They mean to keep her through the winter. They figure she will break." Running Bear's face looked older with each word he spoke. "It's far from her family. It will get cold early. Her family is her life, so they know this is her weakness."

River went into the kitchen to get Running Bear a cup of tea. He'd probably spent hours sitting in this kitchen, chatting with his dear friend. Actually, Fiona did the chatting, and more often than not, Running Bear sat silently. It was their way.

He perched on the bar stool, his shoulders slumped a bit. River put the tea in front of him, rummaged around for some of Fiona's cookies she knew he favored.

He touched neither, but nodded his thanks.

"So now what?" River asked.

"I am not sure."

Tighe came in the back door, glanced at River and Ana, then Running Bear. "What's happening, Grandfather?"

"Fiona is in Montana."

"Montana?" He looked at River, his brows raised. "Wolf's got her?"

Running Bear nodded silently. River looked at both men for a moment, then poured Tighe a cup of coffee and went back to the den. Ana followed, and they sat down to talk privately.

"If Fiona's in Montana, Burke's going to—"

"Don't think about it," Ana said. "The Callahans will figure something out. They did for Taylor."

"We could go get her."

Ana blinked. "Go get her?"

"Sure. We're not Callahan. Wolf would never suspect us." The more she thought about it, the more River was convinced it was a smart idea. "We're both trained bodyguards. We can take care of ourselves."

"You're pregnant," Ana reminded her.

"This is true," River said, "but I haven't noticed it yet. I'm still in fighting form."

"Tighe would lose his mind if you left. He wants you resting."

River nodded. "We wouldn't tell him. Not immediately."

"I want no part of this. None."

"It may not be necessary. Running Bear always has a plan." River thought about that for a few moments. "But Fiona's not staying there for months like Taylor had to, not if I can help it."

"River," Ana said, sounding very worried, "Tighe would freak out."

"That's okay. He freaks out on occasion. It's part of his psyche." River crossed to a window, stared out. "I know she's frightened."

"I doubt very seriously Fiona is frightened. Mad as a hornet, but not frightened. After you've raised a basketball team's worth of boys, you don't scare easily."

"This was what Wolf wanted all along. He knew he couldn't get any information out of the others. It was all scare tactics." River looked up at Tighe and Running Bear as they walked into the den. "Wolf wanted Fiona all along."

"I agree." Tighe nodded, went to rub River's shoulders.

"Don't agree too much," Ana said. "River wants to go get Fiona."

Tighe's hands tightened on her shoulders, then abruptly dropped. "Absolutely not. Out of the question."

Running Bear glanced at her. "Maybe in the spring."

"Spring!" River was horrified. "Why the spring? Fiona can't stay there with those thugs that long!"

Ash walked in, looking depressed. "Whoever took Fiona covered their tracks well. I pride myself on tracking, but I'm not finding much to go on."

"Running Bear knows where Fiona is," River said.

"You do, Grandfather?" Ash looked surprised.

"She is in Montana." Running Bear's eyes were dark with some emotion River couldn't really define.

"Montana? Where they took Taylor?" Ash demanded. "Let's go get her! And this time, we'll burn that shack down. I'm sorry, Grandfather, but we can't go on living in fear."

"Whoa," Tighe said, going to comfort his sister, which River was glad to see. "We need a plan. We can't just go burn Wolf out of there."

"Yes, we can," Ash said. "Yes, we most certainly can! *I* can, if no one else wants to."

"I can, too," River said. "I've got your back. In fact, I'll drive."

Jace and Galen came into the room. "Where are we driving?" Galen asked.

"I want to go rescue Fiona and burn Wolf right out of his lair." Ash's arms crossed, her posture stubborn. River silently applauded her, more than ready herself to drive the truck to rescue Fiona.

"Tonight," Tighe said, "we'll sit down as a family and discuss this. Right now, everyone go back to your posts. No one, and this means you both," he said to River and his sister, "will be doing any sneaking off to do any burning, torching, rescue attempts or any other mission. Is that understood? We need a battle plan, not a herky-jerky attack."

"It's not herky-jerky." Ash glared at Tighe, then turned to her grandfather. "Running Bear, we've always adhered to your rules. We understood we were never to harm Wolf. But this is troubling."

The chief nodded. "Troubling, indeed. But it will not solve the problem of the cartel, and right now, Wolf is the liaison. My son is the devil we know."

River went to warm Running Bear's cup. Tighe followed her into the kitchen. "You will not be going to Montana."

"I'm willing. Someone needs to get Fiona. I'm trained for this, Tighe."

"And you're carrying my children."

"I'm barely showing. Not at all, really. An ounce of stomach I didn't have before."

"It doesn't matter." He pulled her into his arms. "You're not putting my sons in danger."

"Daughters."

"Do we know that?" He leaned back to look at her.

"No. I just feel like torturing you because you aren't already on the road to rescue Fiona!" Tears suddenly sprouted from River's eyes. "Oh, my God, I'm so sorry. I've never been a crier. I have no idea why I'm suddenly crying." She grabbed a tissue from the box on the counter.

"Treading carefully here, but isn't it normal for women to be emotional when they're pregnant?" Tighe asked.

She blew her nose. "I'm a well-trained bodyguard. I'm not emotional. I'm simply annoyed with you."

He smiled, held her against his chest. "Thank you for loving my aunt so much."

"Well, I do." River pulled away from him, not pleased that he was seeing her with her nose running and sounding like a dented trumpet. "I can't bear the fact that they took her. I would trade places with her in a flash! She's too old and fragile to be in Montana with Wolf and his minions."

She blew her nose again and he laughed, kissed the top of her head. "Aunt Fiona's the least fragile person I know."

"She has you fooled."

"I guarantee you she's giving Uncle Wolf fits."

"Good for her. I hope he has an infarction of epic proportions." River looked up at Tighe. "I know the chief doesn't want us to be violent, doesn't want you to exact any justice on your uncle, but I would just like to say that I'm not part of this family. That makes me an obvious rule-breaker." She gazed at him earnestly. "Send me up there, Tighe."

"No. But I can tell that I'm going to have a really interesting married life."

"No, you're not," River said. "I'm not agreeing to marry you until you get Fiona back. I feel quite stubborn about this. It wouldn't be a wedding without your aunt."

"No, it wouldn't." He looked thoughtful. "I'm going to order some dinner for this crowd. Then I want you to rest."

Her jaw dropped. "How can you think about food at a time like this?"

"Easily. No one has eaten all day." He allowed her to move out of his arms, went to poke around in the fridge. "I'm nothing if not practical. I've always been practical."

She followed him to the refrigerator. "I think you're in shock."

"No." He shut the fridge door. "I just know that this will be a long mission. Planning will need to be done carefully. And that requires food."

She sighed. "Why do I get the funny feeling that you're trying to give me a subtle hint that I should take over Fiona's kitchen duties, or else everyone on this ranch will starve?"

He laughed. "No. We're all capable of scrambling eggs for ourselves."

"We really are going to starve." River perched on a bar stool, watched him rifle through the cabinets, searching for containers Fiona had stored. "If you get your aunt back—like, say, tonight, tomorrow—you won't have to worry about your stomach."

"Good point," Tighe said, "but—"

He froze suddenly and looked at her. "This is my journey." He sounded stunned.

"What journey?"

He pulled out some cookies, crackers, fruit. River watched with astonishment as he prepared a large snack for the family.

"The journey I'm supposed to take. I learned about it during my time with Running Bear." He made a small plate for her. "Eat, please."

She didn't really feel like it, but picked up a piece of fruit to pacify him, keep him talking. "The journey?"

"It started on Firefreak."

"Quick journey," River observed with a wink.

He waved a cookie in her direction. "Sarcasm isn't allowed when one speaks of their visions."

"Sorry. Truly." She ate a cherry and then a strawberry. "So, in the beginning, there was Firefreak."

"Actually, in the beginning, there was you." He sat by her, started a different kind of journey leisurely kissing a trail down her neck. "You put me on that bull."

"I was part of the plot to keep you off, if you recall. Continue."

"Believe me, I will." He kissed the cradle of her collarbone.

"Tighe, someone's going to come into the kitchen." Still, she didn't push him away.

"I know. I think it excites me. If I compromise you, you'll have to marry me."

"I think we already compromised each other." Regretfully, she pushed him away. "Can we stick to the journey? Stop trying to change the subject."

"Soup's on!" he called into the den. "Or at least all you're getting to eat without you fixing it yourselves."

The family trooped in, stared at the repast.

"Thank you, brother," Ash said. "You tried. I can tell you made a sincere effort."

Tighe smiled. "Thank you."

"We think we have a plan," Galen said. "Running Bear?"

"I will go," the chief said. "Wolf is my son. He will not harm me."

River saw concern jump into Tighe's eyes. "You're exactly the one he would harm, Grandfather," he said. "I'll go."

"I'll go with you," River said quickly.

"No," he stated, and she bristled.

"Listen, you don't get to have all the harebrained plans in this relationship, Tighe."

"Harebrained?"

"Harebrained. Like riding Firefreak as the beginning of your journey." She glared at her handsome cowboy, whose ego could barely fit in the same room with his body. "Riding Firefreak was an ego thing. You were trying to keep up with Dante. So you hurt yourself, just like your family knew you would, and went and sat in the desert for a few weeks. I'm not sure if you had an epiphany of the soul out there or not, but what I do know is that on this journey to Montana, I am going with you."

Tighe opened his mouth to protest, and she looked at the chief.

"She has a strong heart. She will go with you," Running Bear said.

"She is also pregnant with three babies. Did she tell you that, Grandfather?"

Running Bear smiled. "All the more reason River should go."

"I don't understand," Tighe said as the old chief exited the kitchen. Thunder rattled the windows, though there was no storm outside. "You're stubborn. Do you know that?"

"Not as stubborn as you are," River said. "I consider that a compliment." She slid off the bar stool and headed out the door Running Bear had exited.

"Where are you going?" Tighe asked.

"To pack. See you at first light."

Chapter Nine

"I'm still not sure how I got talked into this," Tighe said as they left New Mexico behind. River sat next to him in a black stretchy skirt she said gave her belly plenty of room to grow, and a cute black lacy top. Her hair was pulled up on top of her head in a bouncy ponytail that made him want to kiss her.

Actually, just about everything about River made him want to kiss her, and then some.

"It's the next leg of that journey you're on," she said. "No worries. We're just taking the journey together. I hope that won't make you feel crowded." She giggled, enjoying teasing him.

He wished her being along for the ride made him feel better. "You should be resting. Your feet should be up, and you—"

"Tighe, this is probably a good time for you to keep those cute little opinions and phobias to yourself," River said, patting his arm, "or this is going to be a very long, very tedious trip."

"I can take a hint."

"That's good news!" She peered at her phone, going over directions. "The route looks pretty straightforward, so let's develop our battle plan."

"I think any plans I ever had went completely out the window." He wondered if it had been wise to make this rescue attempt with no other backup than his pregnant significant other. "I have an idea," Tighe said. "Since I agreed to bring you with me, let's get married in Montana."

"Once we rescue Fiona."

He blinked. "Does that mean that you won't marry me if our mission doesn't succeed?" It had taken Falcon months to get Taylor back home. He didn't think he could wait that long to make River his. On the other hand, it didn't seem he had much choice.

She turned her head and stared at him. "We *will* succeed in rescuing Fiona. If you don't, I will."

"I knew when I first saw you, slinking around Rancho Diablo, walking like a sexy panther, that you were the woman for me," he said, happy to get that off his chest.

"You think I walk like a panther?"

He nodded. "Even though you and Ana have changed your hair color a few times since you first arrived, one thing that hasn't changed about you is that sexy walk."

"Wait a couple more months. I hear a waddle sets in."

He laughed. "You're going to get sexier with every passing body change. I can't wait to see my triplets transform you."

"Your boundless enthusiasm for my pregnancy is very manly."

"It's your determination that warms my heart. The fact that you set a task and do it. Like the night you seduced me."

"I didn't actually seduce you," River said.

"You did. You got me tipsy and had your way with me." He grinned. "Anyway, I believe this journey we're on will bring us closer together. We'll have lots of time to get to know each other on the drive, anyway."

"Yeah, about that," River said, "there's something I need to tell you."

He felt a slight warning tickle, dismissed it. "I'm listening."

"I think I brought bad luck to Fiona."

"Not possible, gorgeous."

"I opened the magic wedding dress bag."

The smile slipped off his face. "I thought you said you didn't."

"Well, I did."

"That doesn't have anything to do with Fiona." His uneasiness grew. "It just means you weren't comfortable with whatever was in the bag." He slid a glance her way. "Am I guessing correctly?"

If he was right, that didn't bode well for him. He drummed on the steering wheel, noted River wasn't swift in answering him. "This getting to know each other on a long drive is going to be a brilliant idea."

"We'll see."

Maybe not that brilliant. "So are you going to tell me what you saw?"

"I believe what happens in the attic, stays in the attic." River looked at him. "Isn't that the rule?"

"I don't exactly know the rules of the attic."

"But you were the one who said the Callahan brides never discussed what happened up there. It was their own personal emotional journey, you might say."

She was turning his own words against him. "You pride yourself on being a rule-breaker. I'm listening if you want to talk."

"It might be bad luck. Perhaps after we find Fiona I'll tell you."

"But suffice to say it wasn't your dream-come-true moment?"

She sighed. "Aren't I supposed to see my handsome prince? Isn't that the wedding tale?"

"I'm not exactly certain on all the ins and outs of the magic wedding dress, but I think it's safe to say that most brides at least have some feelings of warmth and perhaps delight when they encounter their perfect dress. And then I think there's something about the prospective bride—that would be the lady trying on the gown—perhaps seeing the face of her true love." Tighe glanced at River. "You sure you didn't see me?"

"If you were the silent brother, you sure have changed."

"You're avoiding the subject." He felt a huge stone lodge in his chest. "You didn't see me, did you?"

"I didn't see anything. I didn't try it on. I assume that's when the magic occurs. Unless something was supposed to happen when I unzipped the bag." She shrugged. "Nothing did. Maybe you and I don't meet the standards of the magic lore."

With some discomfort Tighe remembered Dante had said Ana had a similar disconcerting experience with the gown. He hadn't paid too much attention to his twin's ravings at the time. "Maybe I should have paid better attention to my brother's misery."

"Probably not. Dante is really happy now. Sometimes it's best not to get involved with sibling misery. Let people figure things out for themselves."

Tighe straightened. "River, do you have any brothers or sisters? Family?" He supposed somebody at the ranch knew all the particulars about her but he'd never heard any details. "I mean, is there a father whom I should ask for your hand in marriage?"

"Tighe," River said, "that's really sweet. But it's not necessary."

Why wasn't it? Because she wasn't going to marry him? There were moments with River when he had to breathe deep, look inside himself, to stay calm. The woman had more twists and turns to throw him off than a river, like her namesake. A long, winding river he couldn't seem to tame. "When we get to Montana I want you to let me take care of everything. On this I insist."

"You just want me to sit here and look pretty?"

"Could you?" He met her gaze. "Just this once?"

"Not likely. I'll probably have your back and still look pretty doing it."

He blew out a long breath of frustration. "It's *my* aunt who is in trouble. You're pregnant with *my* children. You see my problem?"

"Yeah. You've got yourself in a real pickle, cowboy."

She was laughing. Completely confident in her ability to take care of herself, and him, and rescue Fiona, if she had to. And this wasn't the kind of female to whom one could say "Stand down" because *stand down* wasn't in her vocabulary.

It was as if he'd met himself, in female form, only a bit wilder, a little more brave and courageous than maybe he'd ever been. The dark days of war were long behind him now, hidden places he didn't really visit in his soul. Not very often, anyway. He remembered he'd been tough, and was comfortable being in survival mode—but he didn't want River to have to be. "I view this trip as early recon, babe. Reconnaissance. That's it, and nothing more. Once we get the lay of the land, I'm calling for backup. Lots of it. Everything I need to get Fiona out of there. And you're not going to play hero. Not with my babies. You agree to that, or I'm turning around right here, right now."

"Stop the truck."

He pulled off the highway at a beautifully wooded rest stop, switched off the truck. "You okay?"

"I'm fine." She put a hand on his arm, slid it to his chest. "Tighe, I'm not making any promises."

"You have a problem with promises, don't you?"

"The kind you're asking for, yes."

He took that in, allowed himself to drown in her eyes for a moment. "This was a mistake. I should have tied you to Sloan and Kendall's twins so you couldn't follow."

She glared at him. "Still enjoying getting to know me better, cowboy?"

"It had to happen sooner or later."

"Yes, it did. I just want you to know that if I see a chance to grab Fiona, I'm going to do it, and I expect you to rev the engine and haul cowboy butt down the road. Are we on the same page now?"

He gritted his teeth. Never had he wanted to kiss her so badly; never had he wanted to turn the truck around and head back to Rancho Diablo more than now. "I'm not letting anything happen to you."

"And I'm not letting anything happen to *you*." She leaned over, kissed him lightly on his lips. He held very still, enjoying what she was doing to him, not about to move in case she stopped. He never wanted her to stop. But then she did stop, and stared into his eyes. "We're a good team, even if I didn't see you in Fiona's enchanted attic."

"Maybe you didn't really look," he said hopefully,

wanting to keep her close, wondering if he dared pull her to him and kiss her like he wanted to. "You could always try again. See if you get a different result."

"I don't really believe in magic. So I didn't expect to see anything. Trying again won't change that, I think."

He gulped hard, remembering his brother's angst over cursing the wedding gown. "I believe in magic, and spirits, and everything that can't be explained."

She leaned her forehead against his. "I know. It's one of the reasons I'm crazy about you."

His spirit soared. "You're crazy about me?"

"Yes, I am. When you're being normal, like you are right this moment. Not when you start telling me how you think I should do everything. And most certainly not when you try to run my life."

He couldn't help himself. She was so close, she smelled so good and he'd waited so long to be able to touch her that every chance he got was a chance he didn't intend to waste. He moved to her lips, kissing her, lifted his hands to her shoulders and up into that beautiful hair. She was his life preserver, his reason for being—his reason for his journey—and he had no intention of ever letting her go.

If anything happened to her, it would kill him.

"Can I lock you in the truck when we get to Wolf's hideout?" he murmured, after he'd reluctantly pulled away from her sweet lips.

"Put that out of your mind, cowboy. Now get this truck in gear and let's go. We're a team, and you need me."

"I need you," he agreed, and started the engine. He needed her, and his babies, and everything River meant to him.

If he had to kill his uncle to keep his woman and his children safe, he'd do it in a heartbeat.

He heard his grandfather's voice echo *"No"* in his mind, loud and clear and so sharp he glanced at River to see if she'd noticed anything. She was deep into staring at the map on her phone, plotting.

If it meant going against what he knew of life, and the spirits, and even his grandfather, Tighe would take the life of his uncle. To save what he loved most, it might be the only way.

And that's when he knew the truth.

He had to be the hunted one.

Chapter Ten

The lair lay in an area so remote and distant, so shrouded from the main roads, that Tighe was amazed Taylor had lived here for months. Falcon had to have lost his mind while she was gone. Tighe couldn't imagine River being away from him that long.

It probably would do him in.

"This is it." River peered through some high-powered binoculars she'd pulled from her black backpack. "This is definitely the place. Guess who's outside feeding the birds." She handed him the binocs.

He stuck them up to his eyes. "Aunt Fiona. She just went back inside the house."

River nodded. "And just behind you'll see those two female bodyguards Taylor talked about. We know they're the weak link in Wolf's plans. We'll work them over."

Tighe lowered the binocs and stared at the mother of his children. "Where did you get these? They're military grade, with night vision."

She shrugged. "You wouldn't have expected me not to come prepared, would you? *You* didn't, surely."

He had a few guns, a hunting knife, nothing he thought he'd use. Some rope, some other odds and ends, a small explosive device Jace had tucked away in the truck bed at the last minute, saying it was "just in case the opportunity presented itself." Meaning, if he got the chance to lay an explosive and blow Wolf's hideout to kingdom come, the siblings wanted him to press *Blow*. "I've got a few things. Why? What do you mean, you came prepared?"

She opened her pack. "Just a few equalizers."

He looked in it at the array of armaments, his jaw dropping. "You didn't pack any clothes?"

"We're not here for tea and cookies, are we?"

"No, but—" She was going to give him a cardiac event of epic proportions. "You're not on the payroll at the moment!"

"I believe I draw a salary at Rancho Diablo."

"Yes, but I mean, you're just along for the ride, beautiful. Your role is to keep me company, not—" He glanced inside the bag again. "Holy crap, you've got enough stuff inside here to take out a lot of bad guys."

She zipped the bag closed. "We won't need most of it. My specialty is getting in and getting out, sight unseen. That's why I said I want you prepared to roll cowboy butt if I get the chance to grab your aunt."

He swallowed hard. "River, you're going to have to marry me. You need to make an honest man out of me. You're the only woman who thinks like I do."

She laughed. "Don't flatter yourself. I think on a much higher plane. You're too bogged down by worries. Compartmentalizing doesn't appear to be your thing." She got out of the truck.

"Great Spirit," he whispered. He looked out the window at River stretching the kinks out of her back and legs, and felt himself get turned on and fearful all at the same time. "That lady is my path, my life. And the stress just may kill me."

He got out to join her.

"Okay, I think I've got a handle on this now," he said, squatting next to her as she took cover behind a large boulder, spying with the binocs on the wooden cabin surrounded by trees at the top of the muddy road.

"Good."

"Here's the thing." Tighe moved the binoculars from her face so she'd look at him. "This time, right now, you're not a bodyguard. Not *my* bodyguard. You're man number two, and I'm not a chauvinist. Can we agree on that much?"

She smiled. "Now you're catching on."

"Yes. Slowly." He kissed her, because he couldn't stand to look at her lips and not possess them any longer. "We're equals, but you let me have override status on this mission."

"It's your aunt, and your fight. I can agree to that."

"My God, you're sexy." He'd give a million dollars to get Fiona out of there, toss a small grenade into the dump, put Fiona on a plane home and take River to a quiet place in the woods to make love to her until her pregnancy would no longer allow it.

"Focus, Tighe." She handed him the binoculars. "Everything else can wait."

He looked toward the cabin. "There's Uncle Wolf. I'm pretty sure he's made us."

"He made us two minutes ago. That's okay, we weren't really trying to hide. And he was expecting us. We don't want to disappoint him."

Tighe looked at River. "How do you do this?"

"I'm highly trained. And unlike you, my mind is on the mission."

"You've blown my mind so badly it's all I can do not to just sit and stare at you. All I think about is getting you in bed with me again."

"Tell you what." She smiled at him, laid her head on his shoulder. "You rescue Fiona, and I'll leave my nightstand light on for you."

His heart beat hard. "All I have to do to get back in your bed is break into a camp, overcome half a dozen bad guys and a couple of bad girls, and rescue a little old lady? And you'll sleep with me?"

"All night long."

He grinned. "River Martin, I'm madly in love with you. Just remember I told you that." He kissed her one last time, handed her the binoculars and walked into the open field to meet his uncle.

If he was the hunted one, then Fiona should not be the one to suffer.

RIVER WATCHED TIGHE walk away, wondering if facing Wolf down was the best plan. Just to be certain, she got out a gun with a silencer and aimed it toward Wolf. Running Bear might be against shooting his son, but that didn't mean she couldn't do it. She could wing him, give Tighe a chance to retreat.

She lowered the gun. Tighe wouldn't retreat—he would fight. And it wasn't her place to shoot Wolf.

"But I can rescue Fiona." Taylor had told her the location of the bedroom she'd been assigned, as well as that of its window, and how Running Bear had managed to communicate. Getting up, River skirted around through the woods to the back of the house while Wolf's attention was on Tighe. She found the window Taylor had described to her, and peered inside.

Sure enough, she could see Fiona's rubber-soled boots next to the bed, though Tighe's aunt wasn't in the room.

This could be a setup. Wolf would expect them to look for Fiona in the most obvious place. "Which is why we're not falling for the boots-in-Taylor's-room trick," River muttered. She moved to the next room, peeked in the window. Two twin beds, both unmade, were cluttered with a few changes of ladies' clothes. Some shoes and socks lay scattered on the floor. This would be the bedroom of the two women who'd been kind to Taylor, after a fashion. "Messy. It's a wonder Fiona doesn't whip their butts into shape."

River moved to the final window on this side of the hideout. The shades were tightly closed, so there was nothing to see. She wondered if this was Fiona's room, well protected against prying eyes.

"Hi!" a voice whispered next to her, and River nearly jumped out of her skin.

"Fiona! For heaven's sake!" She put a hand over her hammering heart, then threw her arms around the older woman. "I'm so sorry I let you get taken! Are you all right?"

Fiona's eyes twinkled after River finally released her. "I'm fine."

"Good. Come on." She grasped Fiona's hand and pulled her toward the woods, but Tighe's aunt resisted.

"I can't go."

"Why not? Now's your chance! I've already instructed Tighe to be ready for a fast getaway."

"I like that plan!" Fiona shook her head. "Alas, I can't."

"Why not?" River hated to rush the head of the Callahan clan, but if Fiona didn't quit dithering, she was going to toss her over her shoulder and carry her off.

"Because they'll come after us. I heard Wolf discussing the plans with his gang of trolls," Fiona whispered back. "This is a setup."

"I figured as much. It's too easy." River thought quickly. "Tighe's out there jawing with his uncle even as we speak."

"I know. Tighe's brave. Not always the brightest, but always the bravest." Fiona looked satisfied. "It isn't very bright to try to beard Wolf in his den, you have to admit."

"There are a lot of fine points about your family I might be willing to admit, but we should discuss them another time, Fiona. Even if this is a setup, we can go hide in the woods! They won't be expecting that!" River pleaded.

"True." Fiona considered that. "But I can't. If they catch you before we're able to meet up with Tighe, they'll keep you here, too. And that won't be good for those precious babies you're carrying."

"I can't bear to leave you here."

Fiona fastened bright eyes on her. "Now listen, we have no time for sentiment. I need you to take over my committee for the annual Christmas ball. Talk to my friends at the Books'n'Bingo Society. Those three ladies will be happy to help you plan the thing. Be sure you don't forget the advertising on the barn roofs." Fiona tapped her mouth with her finger. "There's only Jace, Galen and Ash left to manage marriages for. I say you advertise Jace this year on the roofs. I guess the ladies would consider him a decent raffle prize."

River glanced over her shoulder. "Fiona, if you're not coming with me, you need to go back inside. I don't want them catching you out here." She gave her another hug. "Are you sure you won't come with me?"

"I'm perfectly happy here. Not as happy as I'd be at home," Fiona said, straightening her shoulders bravely. "I'd rather be in my own kitchen, around my own family, and the children. But Wolf is trying to get to the family through me, and I won't let that happen."

River nodded. "Okay. Go inside."

"Tell Burke I love him." For the first time, Fiona's eyes got a little sparkle in them from unshed tears. "Tell everyone I love them. And they're not to worry about me. I'm a tough old bird. I've handled far worse than Wolf in my life. Be sure they know I expect them to be warriors."

"I will. Go."

River watched Fiona head back around the side of the house, heard a door quietly shut. She needed to sneak back to the truck, check to see that Tighe was getting the best of Wolf. At least she'd seen and talked to Fiona, and that would reassure Tighe until they could think of a good plan to get her out of here.

River carefully retraced her steps, making certain not to leave any trace of a footprint in the loose dirt. Once safely in the woods, she looked out toward the field, saw Tighe and Wolf still soaking up some sun while they chatted—although based on the stiff, angry postures, it wasn't the world's friendliest conversation. Yet it didn't look as if any blood had been spilled or bones broken. River didn't think either man had moved since she'd surveyed the house.

Three minutes later she was back at the truck, crouched down, covering Tighe's back. She held her breath, watching as Wolf turned around, headed back toward the house. Tighe stared after him, his hands on his lean hips, his wide back strong and stubborn.

"Come on, Tighe. Don't stand out there all day catching rays. Let's hit the road and regroup," she muttered.

After a moment, he turned around, headed to the truck. Pretended he didn't remember that she was there. Started the vehicle, backed it up, wheeled it around, giving her enough cover to jump in the passenger side. She was in the truck so fast that he simply made one smooth backup and then pulled away.

"Well done," Tighe said as she tossed her backpack into the backseat.

She kept low so Wolf or one of his many henchmen wouldn't spy her from a window. "Thanks. What were you two shooting the breeze about?"

"Nothing of real interest. Mainly I didn't want him to see you sneaking around the cabin. You nearly gave me heart failure!" He glared at her. "What were you thinking?"

"That while you two were busy reminiscing about old times, I'd rescue your aunt. I found her and I talked to her." River sighed. "But she wouldn't leave."

"I could have told you that," Tighe said, his tone irritated. "This is Fiona we're discussing. She's never going to do what anyone expects or hopes she will. You put yourself in jeopardy! What if you'd been captured?"

River shrugged. "I wasn't worried about that. Now help me think of a way to get Fiona out of there."

"I can barely concentrate! You've got me so rattled I can't string two thoughts together. You're supposed to ride shotgun, not be the spy who loved me!" He sighed, and River thought it was very heartfelt.

"If it makes you feel any better, Fiona looks awesome. I think she's enjoying her role of family plant."

"We did not plant her there to spy on Wolf."

"But she's a counterbalance to his operation, and I think she relishes that."

"There are days," Tighe said, "when I wonder why I couldn't have fallen for a mousy bookworm who only wanted to stay home and cook and bake for me."

"Because the sex probably wouldn't have been as awesome. I'm pretty sure you're not interested in my cooking skills as much as some other skills."

She could tell he was trying not to laugh, despite his aggravation with her. "I do, however, make a mean lasagna, and I've read all the Five-Foot Shelf books—every one. I can keep your interest, cowboy."

"Impressive, and yet in spite of that, I'm still trying to recover from the sight of you creeping up on Wolf's hideout." Tighe let out a long breath. "On the other hand, I find it awesome that you care enough about my aunt that you'd put yourself in danger to rescue her. That's very sexy."

"It is, isn't it?"

"But," he said, wagging a finger as the truck bumped over ruts in the road, "you have to be careful about putting yourself in danger. You have to think of the babies."

"So you prefer me making lasagna and reading *How to Please Your Man* for when you get home at night?"

"Is that so much to ask?"

She laughed. "That sneaky look on your handsome face tells me that even you know you're not going to have that pleasure, cowboy. You'll have to stick with the real me."

"I'm sticking like glue. Uh-oh," he said, and the smiled disappeared off his face. River turned to look at what had his attention.

Four armed men blocked the road ahead.

Chapter Eleven

"Wolf's henchmen," River said. "Run them down."

"I can't do that!" Tighe slowed the truck, came to a halt in front of the armed guards. He couldn't risk getting shot at with River in the vehicle. Tighe was sure Wolf would have the road blocked behind them, as well. Woods stretched on either side of the road, thick and impenetrable. "We're going to have to hope for the best."

He had a sick feeling in his stomach, though. Henchmen carrying AK-47s indicated his uncle meant business.

River pulled her backpack up beside her. "Don't do anything crazy," Tighe warned. "Let me see if I can talk my way out of this."

Even he knew that probably wasn't likely. But if River started shooting, they'd fire back. He shouldn't have brought her with him.

The passenger door jerked open. "Out, little lady," one of the thugs said to River.

"I'm pregnant," she replied. "At this moment, I'm carsick and likely to vomit."

"That sounds like a personal problem to me." He

gestured with his gun toward the jeep hidden off the road. "Take a seat over there, princess."

"Tell my uncle he doesn't want her. He wants me," Tighe said.

"No." The ugly brute with the facial scar staring in the window shook his head with a sick smile. "He specifically said he wanted you to go home and ruminate on your bad manners."

Tighe cursed his softness in allowing River to accompany him. He should have foreseen this moment. His uncle and he had said nothing out of the ordinary to each other. Tighe had asked him to release Fiona; Wolf had said no. The conversation had merely been the two of them circling each other.

"Go, Tighe," River said. "I'll be fine."

She marched off with her backpack. When one of her guards tried to take her arm to help her into the jeep, she shook him off. Tighe swallowed hard, knowing the arsenal she was carrying. River was likely to leave the place in bits and pieces. His stomach clenched and he could barely breathe past the fear in his chest. She was stubborn, she was fiery and she had Fiona as an accomplice.

Nothing good could come of those two ladies being on the loose and in cahoots. And spirits help her if Wolf decided to have her bag searched.

Tighe looked at the goon next to him, studying the scar. "I know who you are. You're Rhein, Wolf's right hand."

"That's right. And you're the nephew that used to be such a ladies' man. Funny thing, but Wolf's just been dying to pick off a Callahan female to drive you boys nuts. And now that you've decided to settle down with

just one lady, that's the lady Wolf gets to hold as a bar-
gaining chip. I call that irony." Rhein laughed out loud.

"Now drive on, if you know what's good for you,"
the guard to his left said. "And don't look back, if you
don't want to make trouble for the little lady and the
old woman."

"I don't suppose you'd take me instead and let them
go?"

The ugly man shook his big head. "Boss man says
he's got the big fish now. The old lady'll break eventually, and she's the one who knows every secret Running
Bear's hiding." He smiled, and Tighe felt ill. "With the
little pregnant lady as a hostage, Wolf's got all the le-
verage he wants. Somebody'll sing like a bird sooner
than later, I reckon. And then we'll know where to
find your parents, won't we? Both sets of 'em. We've
waited years for this."

"River doesn't know anything," Tighe said, trying
not to sound as desperate as he felt. It was eating him,
driving him out of his mind.

"Your lady might not know anything, but the old
lady knows everything. Wolf says there's only one captive with higher value than her, but we don't need to
play that card yet."

Tighe wanted to keep his talkative friend dropping
clues. "Who's a higher value target than Fiona? Running Bear?"

"Wolf wants nothing to do with his father. If he
ever gets the chance, he'll shoot Running Bear dead."

"Seems like a pretty harsh way to treat one's dad."

"Not my problem. I just draw my weekly pay and
do my job. Now, move along, and no heroics. We shoot
heroes on sight."

Tighe glanced toward River one final time, though

he didn't move his head. Didn't want Rhein to suspect her importance to him. River sat in the jeep, tying her whiskey-colored hair up into a tighter ponytail, acting as if she wasn't a hostage, as if it was just another day in an unexciting life.

Trying to keep him calm.

He was anything but.

TIGHE CALLED AN emergency family meeting upstairs in the library as soon as he returned. He'd even sent Ash to locate Running Bear—although he made Jace ride at her side for protection.

As his brothers and sister and Running Bear took their places, he waited, his heart beating hard. Tighe didn't think his pulse had quit hammering ever since he'd driven away, leaving River in Wolf's clutches. He'd sped home, barely stopping for anything, to consult with his family and develop a plan.

The plans they'd had so far had gone horribly wrong.

Running Bear sat in silence, shaking his head when Galen offered him a drink. The rest of them accepted a crystal tumbler of whiskey, their eyes on Tighe the whole time.

"Where's River?" Ash demanded.

"River and Fiona are both with Wolf in Montana." Tighe watched his family take in this news with dismay etched on their faces. "I didn't want to leave either of them. I had no choice. We have to figure out how to bring them home."

"What happened?" Galen demanded.

"I talked to Wolf in person. He said he has no intention of letting Fiona go. She's his ace in the hole for making sure he finds out where our parents, and our cousins' parents, are in hiding. None of us know that information, but Fiona might. At least Wolf's banking on that."

Tighe looked at the chief, but Running Bear's gaze was flat, emotionless, giving away nothing. "His goal, of course, is to make them pay for informing on the cartel. That's what he's been hired to do, and he won't rest until that happens. Eventually, he says he'll take over Rancho Diablo. The cartel has promised him this in exchange for our parents, Molly and Jeremiah, and Julia and Carlos."

"How could you leave River?" Ashlyn demanded. "She's going to be confined without prenatal care!"

"There wasn't an option. I even offered myself in exchange." Tighe wanted to kill Wolf at the thought of River being held hostage. "Trust me when I tell you I've never been so scared in my life."

Ash flew to him, throwing her arms around him. "I'm so sorry!" she whispered, hugging him hard.

He let his sister comfort him for a moment before he moved away. "While I was talking to Wolf, River managed to get to Fiona and talk to her."

"That was brave," Sloan said. "Scary, but brave."

Tighe remembered the startled fear he'd concealed when he'd seen her moving stealthily through the trees. He'd kept his gaze on Wolf, barely allowing his peripheral vision to acknowledge what River had been doing—but his heart had fallen into his boots. "She said Fiona is fine. She says to tell everyone not to worry."

"Not to worry?" Falcon challenged. "Like hell!"

"I want to kill Wolf," Ash said, "Grandfather—"

The chief held up a hand, and she fell silent. "That is not the answer."

"I personally think it would solve all our problems,"

Ash muttered, "at least ninety percent of them. And we could get Fiona and River back!" She gazed at her brother. "What are you going to do, Tighe?"

He remembered River tying her hair back, ignoring her captors. Many women would be scared. Many men, too, up against what she was facing. "I don't know. The part that frightens me is that I know that, carrying triplets, she won't be easily moved forever. At some point, she'll be confined to bed rest." It would be a whole lot harder to rescue her then.

"This is a dilemma," Dante said. "I'm sorry as hell."

Tighe looked at his twin. "River was carrying a backpack full of things I can only describe as bodyguard goodies. I'm concerned that Wolf will search her bag. Either that, or she'll blow the place sky-high."

"I hope she grabbed the charge I put in the truck for contingencies," Jace said. "It's for one of those just-in-case moments, when you want to make a really big exit."

"Oh, great," Tighe said, closing his eyes with exasperation. It wasn't in the truck now, so River had in fact packed it into her little black bag of fun and games. He opened his eyes and glared at Jace. "There's no reason to encourage her, so don't even say that out loud. She's carrying my children!"

"Yeah," Galen said. "You've got to admire a woman like that. Uncle Wolf has no idea what he bit off by taking on Fiona and River. Those two could hound the devil himself."

"I don't want to think about it." Tighe finished his whiskey and Ash refilled his glass in a hurry. The liquid burned through him, bracing him, but not giving him any creative ideas on how to rescue his woman.

I can't even really call her my woman. She's not exactly overly enthusiastic about marrying me.

"I never thought the day would come when I couldn't defend my own family. And there I sat, with no options, while my family, my whole world, went off with a bunch of armed thugs." Tighe felt as if he'd been smashed to bits, stomped by something stronger and meaner than Firefreak.

"We will wait," Running Bear said quietly, and they all stared at him in surprise.

"Wait for what?" Tighe demanded. "I don't have long to wait. River's a couple months pregnant. I need to get her *home.*" *In my arms. Where she belongs.*

"Well, you can't go after her," Ash observed. "You're still limping. Bet you wish you hadn't tried to ride that stupid hunk of meat, huh?"

"I'm fine," he snapped. "I just came home to get backup." Tighe looked around at his brothers expectantly.

"No," Running Bear said. "You're too hotheaded right now. When passions rule, danger is near. Wolf will expect us to come to him. Yet we will not."

Tighe gulped hard, his throat so tight he nearly couldn't draw a breath nor swallow with ease. "I can't agree to that. I'm going back, either alone or with help. If no one here wants to go with me, I'll hire mercenaries."

"No," Running Bear said again. "Time is on our side. Eventually Wolf will make a mistake."

"I don't have time to wait for mistakes! The mistake has already been made, by me." Tighe looked around at his brothers. "What would you do in my place?"

"Listen to Grandfather," Jace said. "He's suffering more than anyone."

Tighe looked at the old chief, realizing he was, indeed, extremely grieved over this situation. He looked older, sadder, no longer serene. His dark skin seemed to sag a bit with age, and Tighe couldn't remember their energetic grandfather ever looking defeated. But it made sense. Fiona was his best friend in the world. They'd been a united front for years, plotting and keeping lots of people alive. Keeping the land alive, and the Diablos safe. Making sure no one ever tore the family apart. "I'm so sorry, Grandfather," Tighe said. "I spoke in haste. Forgive me."

"I understand," Running Bear said. "We always knew the fight would be difficult and long."

That was true. No journey was ever easy. Tighe's Callahan cousins had been fighting the good fight longer than he. For that matter, Fiona and Running Bear had been trying to save the family and the land for even longer, and before that, Jeremiah and Molly, and Julia and Carlos. "I'm sorry," Tighe said again, the words inadequate. He sat back down on the long leather sofa, forcing himself to take a deep breath. "I am hotheaded."

"It's only natural," Dante said. "When family's in danger, the reaction is to rush in where angels fear to tread."

"Still, we need to have a plan." Ash rubbed Tighe's back. "We're just going to have to wait until the right time comes." She looked at Running Bear. "I do agree with Tighe on a couple of things, Grandfather. I don't want Fiona to be up there during the winter. It would be too hard on her. And I don't need to tell anyone that River needs to be here, resting."

They all took that in for a long time. There was no

good answer. Tighe could hear his own heart beating with stress.

"Calm," his sister said. "We all must stay calm. Wolf is expecting us to come back, guns blazing. It's a pretty good trap."

Tighe paced to a window, stared at the dark landscape beyond. There had to be a way out of this he wasn't seeing.

"By Christmas," Running Bear said, "they will be testing each other's patience."

Tighe whipped around. "Christmas! That's five months from now!"

"There'll be no Christmas without Fiona and River," Ash said sadly. "There will certainly be no Christmas ball."

He couldn't worry about holidays and matchmaking balls. "Grandfather, we can't wait that long!"

"How much time until River probably needs bed rest?" Sloan asked Galen, the doctor among them.

"It won't be longer than December. Not with triplets," Galen replied. "Possibly January, if her weight stays down and she stays healthy. We can always ask our cousins how they fared. There are two sets of triplets in their family."

"Christmas," Running Bear said again, more definite this time. "We plan our raid for Christmas. They won't be expecting us then. The roads will be more difficult."

"Can't we make it Thanksgiving?" Tighe asked. "The sooner I get them home, the better."

"If we go now," Falcon said, "people are going to get hurt."

Tighe feared someone was going to be hurt even if they waited. He thought about River's backpack of surprises and thought he was going to lose his mind. "Am I the hunted one, Grandfather?"

Running Bear's gaze settled on him. "Why do you ask me?"

"Because you said the hunted one would bring danger and destruction to the family. And I have."

His siblings stared at him with sympathy. The chief closed his eyes, shook his head before turning his gaze back on Tighe. "I don't know."

"Sure feels like I am," he muttered.

"Oh, brother." Ash laid her head against his shoulder. "You're a prince."

"I'm not a prince. I'm a guy who's lost the only thing he ever wanted."

"But you'll get her back," Ash said. "It just won't be any quicker, I guess, than when Falcon lost Taylor."

"Yeah, but this is my fault. I let River go with me." Tighe played every moment over again in his mind, wondering if there'd been any way he could have stopped Rhein and his men from taking her. There wasn't. He'd done the only thing he could to ensure her safety. He went to stare out the window again, thinking hard. "Where's Sawyer?" he suddenly demanded.

"Watching little Carlos and Isaiah with Kendall," Sloan said. "Why?"

"Just wondering." Tighe watched a tall man ride up on horseback, settle his horse near a tree, tie the reins to a post. "Storm's here."

"Storm?" Dante asked. The family crossed to the window to stare out at their neighbor.

"Reminds me of the night the rock got tossed through our window up here," Galen said. "We never did prove that he didn't do it."

"I was thinking the same thing." The doorbell sounded, and Tighe said, "I'll go see what he wants."

"I'll go with you," Ash said, scrambling to his side. "And I'll bring up a plate of cookies for the rest of you when we come back. We have a lot to discuss."

They went down the long, beautifully carved staircase.

"Brother, you're going to have to keep it together, for River's sake."

"I'll try. But I'm making no promises."

"I figured as much." Ash bounced to the front door, flinging it open. "Hello, Storm. What brings you here?"

Tighe stood behind his sister. Storm eyed them both, his wide, handsome face framed with silver-gray hair and stubble-rough cheeks.

"I've come to offer to sell you the land your aunt Fiona wanted to buy," Storm said. "I feel I've gotten involved in something I want no part of, and this is the only way to make things right."

Chapter Twelve

River was annoyed, and when she was annoyed, she wasn't the friendliest person to be around, which Rhein quickly found out when he tried to carry her backpack.

"Do I look like I need help?" she snapped.

"Sorry," Rhein said. "Didn't know if pregnant women were supposed to carry stuff."

"Look, you're kidnapping me, right?" She stomped toward the house with five men on her tail. The other two—she knew there were seven, because Xav Phillips and Ash had been tied up in the canyons once by what Ash referred to with great disgust as "the seven birdbrains"—were likely off keeping an eye on Rancho Diablo, reporting back to wicked Wolf. "As long as I'm a hostage, don't even look at me. Don't try to help me, don't be nice to me, because I'm not going to be nice to you. Deal?"

"Sure. Whatever." Rhein went off with his band of uglies, and River sat down on the porch alone, irritated beyond belief that she was now good and stuck.

On the other hand, it was a great opportunity for spying. And it would be easy to report back to Rancho Diablo, because in her backpack she had a cell phone. She looked at the surrounding woods and deep violet twilight sky, and shivered a little as cold tendrils of breeze touched her. She had one change of clothes, a couple of pairs of panties and lots of things Wolf wouldn't be too happy about if he knew she was carrying them.

Fiona came out and joined her on the porch. "At least I have company now."

"You were supposed to be rescued. I botched that."

"No need for a rescue. I sort of like it here." Fiona turned her head up to look at the stars just peeking out in the velvety sky. "I keep everybody in line. I've taught the guard girls to cook a little. They're pretty useless otherwise, not trained to Callahan standards as bodyguards, or in general protection. Nobody is allowed to wear their boots and shoes in the house, and everybody has to make their bed. The toilet lid is always to be put down, and no one leaves water spots on the mirrors."

"How did you accomplish all that? They strike me as a pretty thuggish crew."

Fiona laughed. "Listen, I've raised six wild nephews, and have crewed for seven Chacon Callahans. You get the hang of herding cats. Anyway, if my rules aren't obeyed, I don't cook. Or bake. Not one cookie, not one batch of chili. Trust me, nobody wants to go back to the slop they were eating before my coerced arrival."

"That's awesome." River smiled. "Fiona, you amaze me."

"It's easy when you know what people want." The older woman looked at her. "So, I never did hear what happened when you tried on the magic wedding dress."

River wasn't certain how much to tell. There was a fairy-tale element to the Callahans' precious gown, and maybe that was all it was supposed to be: fairy dust and romance. "Not much," she hedged.

"There's never been *not much* that happens with the dress. You might as well tell me. We've got a long time to sit here and rusticate."

River felt a small chill. "How long do you think we'll be here?"

"Well, if I had to guess, I'd say something will either happen quickly, or not till after winter."

River gasped. "After winter! My babies might be born here!"

"Luckily, it's a beautiful place for babies to be born," Fiona said, trying to sound positive. "Although I'm sure it won't come to that."

They couldn't be sure of anything. "I'm not going to try to see the future," River said bravely.

"Wise choice. So, back to the gown. Tell me what happened!"

Fiona looked like a young girl pleading for a treat. River decided to give in gracefully. "I took the dress out of the bag and hung it on a hook so I could unzip the zipper. But when I touched the gown, it changed."

"Changed?" Fiona repeated, her eyes huge.

"It changed into combat gear. Like something a military operative would wear. Your basic little black dress, except very after-midnight casual." River frowned. "I have no idea why."

"Odd," Fiona murmured. "I can't figure that out at all."

"Nor I."

"Well, did you see anyone?" she asked, eager for more details.

"Not a thing. No one and nothing. I was a bit let down," River admitted. "Actually, I was *very* let down."

"I bet." Fiona looked into the distance. "It wasn't in a very cooperative mood, was it? As wedding gowns go, it certainly was being cantankerous. Combat gear, indeed!" She looked at River. "What would a woman who's pregnant with triplets want with that?"

"I no longer try to understand everything that happens at Rancho Diablo. I just accept it and move on. Or try to." River took a deep breath. "As much as I hate to say it, I have a bad feeling about this mission."

"Well, don't. There's no point in having bad feelings. We have to focus on what we need to do." Fiona reached out and took her hand, and River felt the older woman's fingers tremble slightly.

And that's when she realized the toll the situation was taking on Fiona. She was putting on a brave face to spit in Wolf's eye and to control the way they treated her while she was captive. She might be a prisoner, but Fiona had them convinced that they had to please her; hence the clean floors and shiny mirrors. But she was also putting up a brave front for River's sake. Yet her trembling hand gave her away.

"It's going to be fine," River said. "We're Callahans. And we're the good guys." She patted the older woman's hand. "And when you're absolutely ready to go home, Fiona, you just let me know."

Fiona's eyes widened. "What do you mean?"

"I brought a few magic wands with me," River whispered. "I'm pretty sure I can cause enough distraction to give you time to get away."

"I'm not leaving you! You're expecting my nephew's children!" Fiona shook her head. "No, we're in this together, my girl. All for one and one for all, as they say."

"Then if we have to, we'll teach Wolf and his gang of miscreants Christmas carols."

Fiona laughed. "I can just see Scrooge and his seven dwarves singing carols."

River smiled, desperately hoping they wouldn't be spending Christmas in Montana. Christmas should be at Rancho Diablo—with Tighe.

"WE HAVE TO have a Christmas ball," Ash told her brothers as they slumped on the sofas in the library. Four weeks had passed since River and Fiona had been gone, and the mood was very low. Tighe thought they'd never been so dispirited. Falcon, Sloan and Dante had become so overprotective of their wives and children that the wives had finally snapped at them to quit being such horses' asses.

Everyone was on edge.

Yet Tighe thought Ash was right: Wolf had what he wanted. The jewel in the Callahan crown was Fiona— it had to be. She alone, besides Running Bear, knew all the secrets of the vast ranch, and all its holdings. She knew where the fabled silver mine was, and where its treasure was buried. They knew this, too, now, but their aunt was directly in charge of the finances and all the sources of wealth Rancho Diablo held. Therefore, she was the most important fount of information Wolf could have happened upon.

River was just icing on the cake. Wolf knew she was pregnant, and that the fact would eat at Tighe. Which it did, night and day. He didn't think he'd slept decently since the day she'd been taken. He hadn't, and if he had, he would have felt guilty, knowing that River was a prisoner. What man could ever sleep knowing his woman was a captive?

"I don't give a flip about Christmas balls," Tighe

growled. "It won't be a ball without Fiona, and there's no point in pretending it is."

"That's just the point," Ash said crisply. "Fiona wouldn't want us to act like anything is out of the ordinary."

"Everything is out of the ordinary," Galen muttered.

"No one can plan a party like Fiona," Jace said. "I agree. No ball this year."

"Then Wolf wins." Ash stared around at her brothers. "It's about time we try to fill our cagey aunt's boots. We can do it." She took a deep breath, stared at Tighe. "There's no point in sitting around here losing our minds."

"It's not going to get better just because we party." Tighe shook his head, filled with a gnawing agony over what his woman might be suffering. "I'm going back to Montana," he declared abruptly, catapulting out of his seat.

"No!" his brothers all said, and Falcon and Sloan pressed him back onto the sofa. Dante handed him a whiskey, and he gulped it, trying to collect his shattered wits.

"You can't, bro. Trust me, I know it's not easy having your woman gone," Falcon said. "It was hard as hell when Wolf had Taylor. The thing is, Wolf's trying to get to us. This is how he does it. It's a mind game. All he has to do is keep us rattled, and we'll crack."

"I'm cracking," Tighe said. "In fact, I think I'm past cracked."

"I assign you to finding volunteers," Ash stated. "And you can do whatever deep thoughts and meditation and bookkeeping you need to do to consider Storm Cash's offer to sell us the twenty thousand acres across the canyons."

Everyone stared at her. "What?" Tighe said.

"When did you become the head of the household?" Galen asked.

"Since we're all too down in the mouth to be effective," their sister snapped. "Since he's turned pale and thin," she said, pointing to Tighe. "Since nobody can think of anything but the fact that our aunt is being held by the enemy! And River, too!" Ash glanced around the room. "All of us need to keep busy. We have to live our lives. The die is cast, the way Running Bear says it should be. So we're not going to attack. We're not going to try to get them back. We're going to wait for Wolf to come to us, and that means doing what we have to do." She glared at Jace. "I assign you to setting up cooking schedules. We'll all take one day a week. Every night we all do KP," she told Galen.

"That's probably a good idea," Tighe said with a sigh, thinking that if they all had a healthy meal for a change, instead of the thrown-together grub they'd been snatching from the pantry and Fiona's freezer— mainly cookies and pies, and some frozen casseroles— maybe they'd be able to think better. For his part, he'd mainly been on a liquid diet of whiskey, whiskey and more whiskey. Sips here and there, but he'd known when he got up and poured whiskey instead of sugar into his coffee mug this morning that he was going to have to back off the liquid courage.

"Ash has a good idea," Tighe said. "The more I think of it, the better I like it. We'll each take a night of cooking. Basic meals, no desserts, no frills, but healthy, fresh, living food. An occasional salad would be cleansing."

"Oh, boy," Jace said. "Here we go. Dr. Nutrition speaks."

"I'll talk to Fiona's friends at the Books'n'Bingo Society. They'll be able to give us the blueprint for when invitations need to go out. We'll need some victims," Tighe said, considering his brothers. "Who's going to be the grand prize this year at the bachelor raffle? And to what charity will we donate the proceeds?"

"Fiona loves the school and library so much that I say we split it between them," Galen suggested, and everyone nodded. "They always need supplies and equipment. Maybe we won't make enough to buy a roof for the elementary school, like we did last year, but we'll be contributing something."

"That's right." Falcon nodded. "And then Wolf isn't beating us. We can't allow him to cut the lifeblood of Diablo, or Rancho Diablo. That's his goal."

"That's right," Tighe murmured. "The cartel will get to us when we're weak. We have to stay united as a family, and as a community." He felt strength surge inside him as his brothers and sister murmured in agreement. "Great. Then we're together on this. Jace, you're the grand prize. Galen, you're going on the block this year. Who does that leave?"

They all stared at Ash. She went paler than her hair. "Oh, no. Not me. I'll never be raffled."

"Why? We've all had to do our bit to raise money for the town."

She shook her head. "No. You don't understand. None of you wanted to settle down. All of you fought it hard, or did fight it until you got caught fair and square. But I don't want a man."

"Oh, you want a man," Tighe said, enjoying pricking at his sister's shell of superiority for just a second.

"I've got my man," she murmured.

They all smiled at her as she fidgeted.

"You have your man?" Tighe asked. "Are you sure? Has Xav Phillips been around? I haven't seen him in months."

"That's mean," Ash said.

"If you're not spoken for, you're part of the raffle. It's all for one and one for all," Jace said. "That's what Fiona always says."

"Yes, well, she's speaking of the Three Musketeers type of stuff, but I'm surrounded by the Many Stooges," Ash snapped. "I'm not doing it. I'll support all of you while you raise money, but I prefer to man a lemonade stand or something for my contribution."

They all smiled adoringly at their little sister. "You know," Tighe said, teasing her, "maybe we should invite Xav to be part of Aunt Fiona's custom of being raffled off to raise money for Diablo's—"

Ash hopped to her feet, her hands on her hips. "Go right ahead. I'll buy him."

Her brothers whistled and clapped, and roses bloomed in her cheeks. Tighe looked at his family, enjoying the teasing and closeness, but as he looked out the window toward the moon—the same moon and stars that were surely visible in Montana—he wished he could be with River tonight.

A falling star flew across the sky, bright and brilliant as it flamed on its path.

Tighe turned away. He no longer believed in magic, dreams and wishes cast into the air. He didn't believe in spirits, or connections to the elemental or supernatural. He believed in right and wrong, that was all. White and black. Dark and Light. Good and evil. It was a battle he was no longer certain they could win.

And he had very little patience for the journey he was on.

Chapter Thirteen

It was late October when River heard a light tap at her window, likely snow and sleet hitting the glass. She glanced at her watch to find it was nearly three o'clock in the morning. Snow had blown for days in the wild piney woods surrounding the hideout. Fiona had told Wolf's two female guards they had to put in supplies for hard weather, and they'd gone to the store, bringing back everything Fiona wanted. River and she had started cooking, but when Wolf snapped at Fiona from the tension of cabin fever, as well as no Callahans showing up for a rescue attempt, she had retired from the kitchen for a week, not preparing a thing.

Then everybody in the house and bunkhouse gave Wolf the silent treatment, born of deep resentment. River and Fiona had thought it was funny, because they'd stored plenty of snacks in a barrel outside their window. They were doing fine.

The tap came again, a bit louder, and River realized it wasn't sleet. She crept to the window, slowly raising the shade. "Tighe!"

She slid the window up as silently as possible, not easy because it was wood-framed and swollen. He crawled in, and quickly sprayed the hinges of the window with something before closing it. River couldn't wait any longer—she kissed him like she never had before. "You're freezing!" Pulling off his coat, River pressed herself against him.

"I'm fine, babe. No sense in getting you cold, too." He pushed her away, and pulled off one of his boots. She helped him with the other one, and then dragged him into her bed to warm him.

"You've been outside for a long time," she murmured against his throat. They held each other tightly, and after a moment, his hand stole to her rounded belly.

"I've been there a few hours, waiting for the right moment." He kissed her forehead. "I don't want to endanger you."

"I doubt anyone will notice. They're all upset with each other because they haven't had a decent meal in a week." She giggled against Tighe's chest, loving how it felt to be in his arms again. "Fiona hasn't cooked. She's training Wolf to ask how high when she says jump. The whole gang is about to mutiny because they're hungry. Fiona says they have no survival skills."

"What have you been feeding my babies?" Tighe murmured against her hair.

"We stocked up on healthy goodies, which are hidden in a barrel outside in the snow. They've gotten pretty lax about keeping tabs on us because they're so unhappy. You Callahans haven't ridden to the rescue, and now the weather is harsh for living in this cabin. Wolf doesn't want to pay heating bills, so we're surviving with log fires. But that's only in the den."

Tighe's hands circled her belly. "I brought you prenatal vitamins."

"I have some. The girl thugs bought them for me. Fiona told them to sneak them in and she'd make her special muffins. But thank you." River kissed his chin, then his lips. He hesitated for a moment, then kissed her long and sweetly. She sighed against him. "It's really not that bad here. I guess because Fiona's with me."

"I don't like the thought of you being cold and not having medical care." His hands stole down to her bottom, cupping her against him.

"A midwife comes out every two weeks. And I'm never cold."

"It's like an iceberg in this place. Almost as cold as outside."

"I got to a certain point in my pregnancy where I'm warm all the time. In the night, I kick off all my covers and lie on top of them. I wish I had a fan, I really do. I'd blow it on me constantly."

"That's my boys," Tighe said. "Raising your body temperature."

"Maybe. I'm like a polar bear." Now that she'd warmed him a bit, she wanted to hear the plan. "Why are you here? Are you rescuing us?"

"No. Not yet. Running Bear says maybe after Christmas." Tighe kissed her forehead. "He says Wolf's minions aren't stir-crazy enough. But this storm is going to dump four feet of snow, and then the nerves will really start to fray around here. That's when they'll make mistakes."

River was a bit crushed. Yet she also understood. "I hope it can be by Christmas. The midwife says I'll probably be on absolute bed rest by next month."

Tighe raised up on an elbow. "Okay. Then I'm busting you out of here."

"I'm not leaving Fiona! And if I leave, Wolf will be angry. He might take it out on her." River slid her hands into his pants, feeling his warmth and his strength.

"Whoa," Tighe said, "none of that, young lady."

He tried to remove her hands, but she put them right back, holding the part of him she wanted to hold, while she kissed his mouth, feverishly luring him to make love to her. If she couldn't be rescued, then she definitely wanted him to kiss her, hold her, romance her.

"You're coming with me."

"I will not." She pulled him free of his jeans, massaging him. He groaned, so she kept doing exactly what she was doing—tempting him.

"I brought you a cell phone," he said, making a last-ditch effort to resist her. He tried to put himself back in his jeans, but she'd gotten him into such a state that nothing was fitting in place easily.

"I have one." She climbed on top of him, straddled his stomach, kissed his chin.

"You have a cell phone?"

"Yes. Didn't I tell you? It's in my bag of tricks."

The conversation was conducted in whispers, but River thought that if Tighe could yell at her at this moment, he probably would. He seemed so dumbstruck. Though she couldn't see him in the dark—turning on a light might alert the night watch—she could feel that his body had stiffened. Yes, he was a bit annoyed.

"If you have a cell phone, it would have been nice if you'd texted us how you were doing."

"I could have," River said, noticing that his hands had crept back to her hips. She wore a stretchy pair of pajama bottoms that were light and thin, and a matching top. It wasn't fancy, but for modesty's sake in a house full of eight men and two strange women, she'd wanted pajamas.

Tighe played with the elastic, almost seeming to ignore her bare skin.

"I could have texted, but I was afraid they've got some kind of communication device that looks for cell messages and phone calls. It's not that hard to trace such activity. I never dared to switch the device on. They don't know I have it."

"Smart," he said gruffly. Then his hands slid around to her stomach once more. "You definitely have to leave with me. I can't risk you needing medical help that this area can't provide, especially under Wolf's auspices. This might be a high-risk pregnancy. I can't imagine that having triplets isn't."

She worked him entirely free of his jeans. "I'm not leaving Fiona. And that's that. End of discussion."

"Then she'll come with us."

Her man was dreaming. He was talking big. This was the same guy who'd tried to ride Firefreak when he lacked the skills—according to his siblings—to do so. "No, Tighe," she said, and then did what she had to do to make him forget all about rescue attempts.

River's belly was huge! Tighe had kissed every bit of her once-flat stomach, astonished by the size his sons had stretched her to. And matters were only going to get worse. His growing boys weren't going to stop supersizing. It seemed to him that she was the shape most women were at the nine-month point of a single pregnancy.

In fact, he shouldn't have allowed her to make love to him. That was not a good idea. But her soft hands had been so busy, teasing and tormenting him, and he'd missed her so terribly. She'd moved so quickly, straddling him, that he couldn't resist. He felt comfortable about her taking things at her own pace; still, he'd worried that pleasuring her would bring on an early delivery.

She'd laughed at him, and taken his mind right off anything sane.

Now she slept in the crook of his arm. He hated that he had to leave. An hour had passed; there was no reason to tempt the devil. Tighe got up, kissed her goodbye. Kissed his sons goodbye. "I'll be back in a couple of days. Be ready. Tell Fiona, too."

"But Tighe—"

He put a finger against her lips. "Just this once, I want you to say, *'Whatever you want, darling.'*"

"No one talks like that," River said, and giggled.

"Try it. It's my fervent desire to hear those words on your sweet lips."

"I'll do whatever you want."

"Darling."

"Darling." She giggled again, and he wished he could see her face.

Within a week, they'd be back at Rancho Diablo. With a new moon, they'd celebrate Thanksgiving together, as a family. Then he'd put River in a rocker and make her stay still as a bowl of fruit until his sons were born.

He went out the window and disappeared into the swirling snow.

TIGHE RETURNED TO Rancho Diablo for a rescue party. He went to Ash, because he could trust her to be up for an adventure. "I've got to get River out of there."

His sister turned to look at him from her perch atop the bunkhouse. She'd had binoculars glued to her face, peering toward the canyons. It was a great vantage point, but he was pretty certain she was looking for Xav Phillips just as much as any trespassers.

"What are you talking about? Running Bear isn't ready."

"I saw River last night. The chief's going to have to be ready."

"How did you see her?"

"I staked out the cabin for a few days, figured out the routine and which window was hers." He shrugged. "A big storm moved in, and I took advantage of the situation."

Ash's eyes were huge. "Running Bear is going to gnaw on you for that."

"I don't care. River's enormous. She'll be on bed rest soon. We've got to get her out of there. Fiona, too. River says Wolf's men are fighting among themselves, and Fiona's not feeding them right now. They're like hungry animals."

Ash smiled. "Sounds like Fiona has everything just the way she wants it. Everybody eating out of her palm." His sister shook her head, the smile fading. "But I want no part of what you're planning. Not unless you talk to Running Bear first."

"Ash. River is my woman, and she's carrying my sons. Or my daughters." He didn't care which; he just needed her home safe. Tighe took a deep breath. "I'm getting her out of there. I'm getting her real medical care. This is a matter of my family's lives. My wife's life."

"You're not married," Ash said, with a sneaky smile.

"I'm married in my heart. And River's coming home."

"You talk to Running Bear and tell him the problem, and I'll help you any way I can. I promise." She patted Tighe on the back. "Poor brother. I know this is so hard for you."

"Not hard on me like it is on Fiona and River." He felt terrible about that. "The cabin is freezing. There's no heat. River's brave, says her body temperature changed with the babies and now she's hot all the time, so she's fine. But what if Fiona gets pneumonia? Or River?" He was worried sick. "It can't be healthy to live in those conditions. And though Fiona has everybody doing house chores, it's not like being here."

"I'm so sorry." Ash laid her head on his shoulder. "When Running Bear gets back, discuss it with him."

"Where is he?"

"He's gone somewhere. I don't really know where. I have my suspicions, but if I'm right, he's on a mission. My guess is he's gone to visit the unmentioned part of our family tree. Might not be back for a while. Obviously, we didn't foresee you trying to move up the timetable on the rescue."

Tighe's heart felt as if it might beat out of his chest. "I don't have that long to wait. It's got to happen now." He climbed down the ladder from the roof and headed to find Dante and the rest of his brothers. He and River would be at an altar in the next few days if he had to stop and marry her in Montana on the lam from Wolf. Tighe had looked it up. There were very few restrictions on getting married in that state. No blood work. It could be done.

Or Running Bear might return, and could do a traditional wedding blessing.

Tighe's brothers were out handling their duties. They'd be back by early twilight. It'd be easier to herd them all into the library and state his case then.

Maybe he'd go hunt up that stupid wedding dress

while he waited for their return. He wanted to see what it was that had freaked River out.

Had any of his brothers or cousins laid eyes on the fabled magic wedding dress while in its ephemeral cocoon?

Was it to be handled only by hopeful brides seeking knowledge of their one true love—or could a man touch it? Would it still be a supernatural gown, or would merely holding the charmed fabric turn him into a gargoyle?

It was time they all stopped tiptoeing around the bewitching fiddle-faddle Fiona endorsed. There was no such thing as magic. The thing was, they'd drunk in the stories and the mystery and the mysticism.

He silently crept up to the attic, even though no one was in the main house. At the top of the stairs, he flipped on a lamp and closed the door behind him. Then he went to the closet where the gown supposedly hung, and took a deep breath before looking inside.

There was the shimmery white garment bag, just as he'd always heard. It did seem to twinkle a bit in the dim closet, but that was just his eyes adjusting to the low lighting.

He brought out the bag, hung it on a hook. Stepped back, pondered what he was hoping to learn.

"All right, dress," he muttered. "You're just a fable in this family, a story that was created to get anxious brides to the altar."

The bag twinkled at him. He held his breath and took hold of the zipper.

Chapter Fourteen

There was nothing there.

Tighe stared at the empty space where a magic wedding dress should be. This made no sense. It wasn't at the cleaners, because Fiona wasn't here to take it. No doubt she'd had it properly put away after Ana's wedding to Dante. Yet River had told him she'd seen it. He couldn't think of a single reason that the gown would be out and about without its special garment bag.

This wasn't good.

The thing was around here somewhere. He just had to find it. He'd put it back in the bag, and when he brought Fiona and River home from Montana, everything would be as it should be.

He searched the attic, then every room of the huge house.

The dress was nowhere to be found.

Ash approached him with a puzzled look when she found him rummaging through the basement. "What in the world are you doing down here, brother?"

"I'm looking for something."

She glanced toward the long scar in the floor where the Rancho Diablo silver treasure was hidden.

"No," Tighe told his sister. "It's not there. I wouldn't dare dig anything out of that hole."

"What's not there?" Ash asked.

"The Callahan wedding gown."

Ash blinked. "What Callahan wedding gown? The magic wedding dress?"

"I refuse to call it that," Tighe said. "I don't believe in magic."

Ash shook her head. "Why would it be in the basement?"

"Because it's not in the attic," Tighe explained.

"Of course it is." Ash gave him an impatient look. "Typical male. Can't find anything that's right at hand, in the most obvious place."

"Fine," Tighe said. "Go see if you can find it."

Ash jutted her chin into the air. "I will."

She trotted up the stairs. He went into the kitchen to see who was making dinner tonight. All seven of them had been assigned dates on a dry-erase board, and if anyone needed to swap their night, they erased their name and exchanged with their substitute.

"Blast. It's Galen's night for dinner. That means sloppy joes. I think that's all he knows how to make."

Tighe heard Ash's feet on the stairs. "It's up there, you dork," she said, coming into the kitchen.

He was stunned. "In the bag?"

"Yes. The garment bag is there."

"But did you look in it? Actually unzip it?"

Ash pulled some of Fiona's cookies from the freezer. "I did not."

Tighe looked at his sister. "Then how do you know it's there?"

"Because the bag is there. Where else would the dress be?" She put some cookies on a tray. "I can't unzip the thing, Tighe. It would be bad luck for me to see the dress before my time comes. But I felt the bag. It's in there." She looked pleased by her cleverness.

"Something is inside?"

"Yes. It's definitely a wedding dress. It's kind of long and heavy, and a little poufy."

Tighe shook his head. "It doesn't make sense. I tell you the bag was empty. I unzipped it and looked inside, and I don't believe in magic, so it didn't bother me at all to take a peek. And what was in there was nada."

She studied him curiously. "I realize this is a dumb question, but what exactly were you doing rummaging through the magic wedding dress bag?"

"What do you care?"

She hopped onto the counter and munched her cookie. "Well, it's not the typical thing a man does. Not even you. That type of behavior strikes me as a bit desperate."

He sighed. "Ash, I just wanted to make certain it was there, okay? So that when River comes home, she can wear it and see me in a vision and sit around the fire with the other Callahan brides and tell magic wedding dress campfire stories, all right?"

"You're truly weird. Anyway," Ash said, jumping down off the counter, "if you don't believe me, go back up there and see for yourself, if you have your panties all in a bunch about it being here for River. I haven't heard that she accepted your proposal, but if you're looking for a good luck charm, go ahead and get it off your chest. It's there."

He trudged up the stairs, feeling a bit of an ass.

The bag wasn't in the closet. Wasn't anywhere to be found in the attic. Nor was there a shimmery dress suited for a bride. "Nuts," he muttered. Ash was playing a heckuva trick on him. She'd hidden it, and was downstairs sniggering, just waiting for him to come jogging down the stairs with "his panties in a bunch."

He was a little tired of being the source of family fun. So he went down the stairs, decidedly calm, and not looking like a man who was having a Callahan prank played on him.

"Find it?" Ash asked.

"Yes, I did," he said, and kept walking through the den.

"I told you. I don't know why men have to make everything so hard." She disappeared into the kitchen, and Tighe took his bad mood upstairs into the library, to wait on his brothers to show up.

Magic wedding gown or not, they were going to help him enact the perfect, foolproof rescue for River and Fiona.

He'd worry about what had happened to the erstwhile dress later. There would be some explaining to do once his chosen lady and Fiona returned, but for now, he couldn't worry about dresses.

He had to get his bride home first.

"THIS RESCUE PARTY is going to have to start earlier than expected." Tighe looked around at his brothers and sister, who were sitting on various chairs and couches studying him with grim faces. "River is huge. There's no way she can be moved if we wait until Christmas to raid Wolf's hangout."

Galen spoke first. "Overlooking the fact that you went off post without notifying any of us, and also overlooking the fact that Running Bear specifically told us to stay away, and that you could have gotten caught—" his eldest brother glared at him "—you're not a doctor. How can you tell River's going to need to be on bed rest soon?"

Tighe gulped, remembering River's stomach as she lay on top of him. "I think my babies are going to be linebackers. Her stomach pokes out a good, well, like this." He gestured with his hands to show the size to which River's tummy had grown.

His family appeared to be suitably impressed.

"She hasn't had proper medical care," Ash pointed out. "There's every chance River could soon require high-risk assessment."

Tighe looked at Sloan. "You had the first set of twins. How long was it before Kendall needed to be in bed?"

"She lasted a good while," Sloan said, "but River's carrying one extra. I say we raid."

"I do, too," Falcon said. "We have nothing to lose by bringing her home early."

"Besides," Jace said, throwing his two cents in, "it's not like we all haven't had missions moved up or back on us. We've gone into rough places at the drop of a hat, based on new intel that's been provided to our commanders." He shrugged. "I vote we raid."

"I'm in the mood for a hunting party," Ash said. "I miss Fiona. And River. Fiona's too old to be hanging around without sufficient heat." She frowned. "And frankly, it gets right up my nose that Wolf has any of our family!"

Galen nodded. "Agreed. The time has come."

Tighe felt a sudden chill at his brother's words. *Am I the hunted one, leading my family into the foretold danger and destruction?*

He was caught in a horrible snare. Either path he chose, there was danger.

And he had not forgotten that his chosen bride had a goody bag filled with incendiary party favors with Wolf's and his merry band's names on them. Tighe knew River well enough to suspect she'd throw quite the party on the way out. He closed his eyes. *I'm marrying a warrior. She scares the hell out of me—but I kind of like it, too.*

"Have any of you ever wondered why Callahan men choose to fall for such headstrong women?" he asked.

"I know exactly why," Dante said. "First of all, that's the way we like them. But I'll remind you that I spoke into the wind a blessing on all my brothers, that you would each have a long and arduous chase to get your woman tamed." He looked very satisfied with himself, and they all booed him. "As it's spoken, it shall be done," he reminded them. "All blessings can come to pass."

"Thank you, Oracle. Can you please go back to minding the well or the River Styx or whatever you do in your spare time? We have a rescue to plan." Tighe looked around at his family. "When do we leave?"

"Zero three hundred hours," Ash said. "Set your watches against the clock on the wall. And may I remind everyone that this is a secret mission? I think we can all agree that Grandfather would not be pleased. It's best if we keep this journey to ourselves."

At the word *journey,* Tighe felt that strange breeze of fate blow across his soul once more. He shivered, and set his watch.

AT THE EXACT appointed time, they piled into two vehicles, one a truck comfortable enough for all of them to ride in, and the jeep for backup. One of the vehicles would be used to block the road leading from the hideout, and the other would be used to carry Fiona and River away from danger.

Tighe was more nervous than he'd ever been. He wished he could get a message to River, but she might be right: they might have some kind of device that picked up cell signals. It wasn't worth risking it. Wolf was very experienced at this type of warfare. He was financed by people with deep pockets, and the equipment necessary to achieve their goals.

But Wolf would never achieve his goal as long as there were Callahans at Rancho Diablo. Tighe's temper boiled a bit, the same temper he'd been holding back ever since Fiona had been kidnapped, and which had overheated when River was taken. He couldn't wait to exact revenge on Wolf and his gang.

Tighe and his siblings had left foremen at the ranch on lookout, telling them that not one soul, not even a family friend, was to step foot on the property while they were gone.

Tighe hoped it was enough. The foremen were to keep plenty of activity happening on the grounds so that it looked as if the family was at home, the ranch fully staffed, the place bustling.

"What are we going to do about Storm's offer?" Ash asked. She rode beside him in the jeep, following the truck.

"I don't care. That's Running Bear's and Fiona's issue."

"They think we don't know that Storm bought the land. Remember? We're all supposed to be eager for it." Ash stared down into a bag she'd packed for the trip, pulled out a water bottle for each of them. "I think if we buy it, they'll be disappointed. It'll be like opening presents before Christmas Day."

"I can't think about land right now." Tighe was going over every single detail of the plan they'd elaborately and meticulously laid out last night. They'd gone through every scenario that could possibly occur, and then some that couldn't occur unless a meteor struck the earth. But he wanted nothing left to chance.

"Look!" Ash exclaimed.

He glanced over at her window. A shadow raced alongside them, a man on a mustang, his hair blowing wild and free behind him. "Holy crap," Tighe said.

"It's Grandfather," Ash said. "We should have known we couldn't get away with sneaking off on him."

The shadow disappeared. She glanced at Tighe.

Their gazes met, and neither one of them spoke about what they'd just seen. They looked back at the road in front of them, and tried to remain calm.

Running Bear was with them—in spirit.

Chapter Fifteen

River knew the moment Tighe returned to the hide-out. It wasn't obvious to anyone else, likely not even Fiona. But River heard a wolf howl long and loud, and she knew Tighe had come back for her.

Which was a good thing. She'd begun to feel some stray aches and pains that seemed unlike the previous ones, which came and went without a pattern. These seemed more rhythmic, and not as random.

"Hang on," she told her babies. "Daddy's here."

The babies settled at the sound of her voice, maybe her words. She didn't know. They seemed to shift a lot more now, probably searching for space. She'd be glad to get to a real doctor and learn what was happening with her beautiful children.

She looked in her backpack, made sure everything was ready. The cabin was cold enough that she worried the guns might need cleaning or oiling, but there was no way to address that without putting herself in a position to be caught.

She'd opened her backpack only twice since she'd been here, each time when she was tempted to plug in her cell phone and send Tighe a text. The nights had been long; sometimes fear had descended upon her.

She hadn't given in to it. But it pressed on her, as she was sure it had on Fiona. River tried to learn from the older woman's brave face, and wore her own consistently—but the nights grew long without Tighe's arms to hold her.

Once she returned, she was going to marry him, magic wedding dress or not.

Almost as if she conjured it, it appeared on her bed, beautiful and shimmering with love and magic. "Oh, my goodness," she murmured. "Oh, you are so beautiful!"

She couldn't fit into it now, of course. Even magic wedding dresses couldn't accommodate a belly the size of hers. The only clothes she wore these days were two pairs of sweatpants—men's—that Wolf's women had bought at a Walmart for her. In fact, the sweatpants and tennis shoes she had were hardly appropriate for making an escape through mounds of snow, but she'd manage somehow.

The dress twinkled encouragement at her. "May I touch you?" she said out loud, and the wedding gown threw off a few sparks of iridescence in response.

River ran her fingers over a cap sleeve, touching the delicate lace and diamante sparkles. Tears jumped into her eyes as she gazed at the beautiful dress she would one day wear. "Thank you," she murmured. "Thank you so much for letting me know that I will be a true Callahan bride one day."

The dress glowed with an evanescent quality, and River grabbed her cell phone. "May I take a picture? I want to remember everything about you until the day I finally get to put you on."

She didn't know if photos were allowed before the wedding day. But the garment didn't disappear, so

River plugged in her phone and took two quick snaps, making sure she'd captured the image.

She smiled when she saw her dream dress photos. "Thank you," she said again. "I'm so happy to know that I'll have such a lovely dress to wear when the time comes."

The dress sparkled, emitting a few beams of light, then suddenly disappeared.

In its place was the black ensemble she'd seen in the magic wedding dress bag: a long-sleeved thermal shirt, plus black pants made of some kind of thick fabric suitable for braving the cold. The boots were black and lug-soled, reaching to the knee. A waterproof black coat completed what looked very much like weather-appropriate military gear.

River wiped her tears and tried the clothes on. They fit perfectly, the shirt not too small for her newly large breasts, the pants comfortable enough for her bigger belly.

Now she understood what she'd seen in the magic wedding dress bag.

"If this is the work of my fairy godmother," River said, "I want to thank you for being so flexible and considerate. This is perfect!"

She wished Fiona had warmer clothes. Montana was much colder than they could have imagined, and the cabin was icy much of the time. She'd worried so much for Fiona.

It was high time to get the Callahan aunt home.

River checked her backpack one last time, ready for whatever was about to unfold.

THE CLOSER THEY got to Montana, the more Tighe worried. River, the babies and Fiona were the first worry, but the fact that he'd dragged his siblings into this mission, compromising their safety and their families—those brothers who had young children and wives—cramped his gut. Though they'd gone over and over the plan, anything and everything could go wrong with even the best attack and rescue operation.

He breathed deep, focused the way Grandfather had taught him. Tried to think about the power of the forces that had brought them to this moment. Some things were out of their control—and others were in their control. It was up to them to walk the proper path.

His hatred for Wolf kept him in a dangerous place. Sometimes he dreamed of killing his uncle—dark dreams of violence that shattered his sleep. Tighe always felt the evil knocking, just beyond the door of his subconscious.

"This is the town," Ash said. He felt his sister's gaze on him. "Our brothers are slowing down, so they must mean to turn off before entering, likely so no one will see us and warn Wolf." She studied Tighe. "Are you all right? You haven't said a word for the past hundred fifty miles."

He was fine—and not fine. "I'm just ready."

"Good." Ash rolled down the window, and frosty air hit him in the face. It felt good circulating in the jeep, waking him to the bitter cold. "We made it here in record time, considering the weather."

Night was falling on the small town, the tree-lined mountains in the distance already shrouded in darkness. They'd driven straight through, with very few stops. Gas, occasional bathroom breaks, that was it. They were trained to focus on the mission and ignore weakness in their bodies. Well-schooled first by life in the tribe and their grandfather, and then excellently trained in the military, they would work as a team until the mission was accomplished.

Ash put the window up. "I'm going to pour some coffee from the thermos. Want some?"

"Sure." The coffee would be lukewarm or cold now, but that wouldn't matter.

Suddenly his mobile phone binged, alerting him that he had a message. He glanced at his cell, stunned to see that the message was from River.

Are you coming?

"It's River. She wants to know if I'm on the way." He looked at his sister. "What do you think?"

"It's a trap." Ash shook her head. "I wouldn't reply. What if Wolf found the phone on her and forced her to send the message?"

Exactly what he'd wondered.

"It won't do her any good to know, anyway," Ash said. "If she knows we're close to starting the operation, she'll be nervous. At least if she doesn't know, she might rest until we make our appearance."

He nodded. But it was hard. He wanted so badly to tell her that he was on the way. To ask how she was doing, ask about the babies.

After tonight, it would be all over. The hell they'd endured for the past several months would be a nightmare past. They would be together for the holidays, as a family.

He closed his eyes and listened for any words he might hear in his mind, any directions for the journey he was about to undertake.

Silence.

RHEIN CAME TO get her, the scar on his face standing out against his dark skin. "Wolf wants you."

She looked at him, unafraid. She wore the jogging outfit and tennis shoes she'd always worn. When the time came, she would dress in her new clothes—her version of a fairy godmother's gift—and she would be ready to get Fiona and go home. "Fine."

She followed Rhein to the sparsely furnished den. A tiny fire burned in the fireplace, not enough to warm the room. Otherwise the space was totally dark. Even the shades were drawn. River stood in front of Wolf, not speaking.

"I've just talked to Fiona." Wolf's eyes glittered in the small, dark room. "Despite the fact that I question her every day, she refuses to give any information about Jeremiah's and Carlos's whereabouts."

A snake of fear jumped into River's veins. Fiona had never told her that she was being questioned often by Wolf. River glanced nervously at Rhein, and the big man stared her down.

"Well, we must work with what we've got." Wolf stood up, placed a hand on her stomach. Purely by reflex, River kicked him hard in the shin, stunning everyone, including herself.

He sank into the armchair by the fireplace, his eyes closed. Rhein snatched her arm in a viselike grip.

Wolf took a deep breath after he'd rubbed his shin. "As I was saying, we must work with what we've got. Rhein will show you to your new room."

River jerked against the thug's arm as he pulled her toward the front door. Horrified, she realized he was removing her from the house. "Where are you taking me?"

"To another location," Wolf said, following behind, prodding her forward when she dug in her heels.

She couldn't leave this house. Tighe would be here anytime to rescue her. "Don't make me leave. I need to be with Fiona."

"That's precisely your worth. I thought time away from her family would break the old woman, but she thinks she's running the show around here." Wolf stood back, watching, while Rhein guided her into the off-road vehicle with less than gentle hands. "The old lady is locked in her room now. No one will be happy for a while. They'll miss her cooking. But I'm not going to be happy until I have the information I'm seeking, so," Wolf said, his gaze on River, "she's going to get plenty of time to think about being more forthcoming with that information."

"Fiona will never say anything," River declared.

"She very well might, once she realizes you've been taken to that shack up there," Wolf said, pointing to a cabin high atop the mountain, surrounded by woods, barely visible from their location. "That's our lookout house, a guard shack, you might say. You'll be there for some time, I'm sure, so get used to it. There'll be a team to keep an eye on you, make sure you're being a good girl." He stepped back from the vehicle, and Rhein got behind the wheel. "It's very, very difficult to get to. People have gotten lost in those woods and never been found. In these conditions, you wouldn't last long."

River's blood chilled. Tighe wouldn't know she'd been taken from here. She looked up at the shack that was to be her new home. "Please let me stay here."

"No," Wolf said, "we've got to break the old lady down somehow. The best way to do it is for her to know that you and those little babies are suffering in the cold. No heat or electricity up there, by the way. For your sake, I hope Fiona breaks quickly."

"I hope she never breaks," River retorted. "I need my backpack. It's got my only change of clothes in it." Her magic wedding dress clothes were tucked in the back of the tiny closet. She hadn't wanted anyone to glance in the room and see them. Wolf's gang would know she hadn't come with them, and would instantly know Tighe was close by.

Wolf shook his head. "In a day or so, when the old lady realizes you're stuck with nothing, she may loosen her tongue a bit. Until then, Rhein will take good care of you. And I'll tell the girls to make certain your backpack is put away safely."

River glared at Wolf, hating him more than she'd ever hated anyone. "If anything happens to me, Tighe will make you regret it."

"Live by the sword, die by the sword, I always say," Wolf said. "Rhein, get her out of here."

IT WAS COLD on the mountaintop, colder than she'd ever been in her life. The sweats she wore weren't suited for snow and icy conditions, nor were the tennis shoes.

"It's going to be a bit chillier here than the hideout," Rhein said as he parked the vehicle behind the shack, where it couldn't be spied from the road or sky.

"Don't talk to me," River shot back.

"It's pretty lonely up here. You'll want to talk to someone soon enough. You and the old lady are quite the chatterboxes."

"Are you deaf?" River snapped. "I said don't talk to me."

"All that prissiness is going to get you nowhere."

He walked her to the back door, opened it. "Welcome home."

She ignored him and went inside. The chill of the place practically smacked her in the face. It was dark and felt damp from lack of heat. Her breath made puffs in the cold air.

"If you're nice, I'll see you get a blanket. But all that attitude's going to make sure you just sleep with sheets."

She looked at Rhein, let him know with her gaze that she considered him reprehensible. "I'll be fine."

"There's your room, princess." He pointed down the hall.

She marched into it, closed the door, locked it. Curled up on the ratty cot with the nasty gray sheets and began to plan her escape.

Chapter Sixteen

The Callahans crouched, well hidden by the woods, and gazed at the hideout. Tighe studied the opportunities for entrance and egress, and looked for signs of recent activity. He was ready to bust in there now and grab River and Fiona, so he had to force himself to think clearly, logically, rationally. Any mission had to proceed according to the best-laid plans, carefully crafted with painstaking detail.

But the wait was hard.

"Four lookouts," Jace said, staring through binoculars, "and a fresh set of tire tracks with chains leading to the west."

"And up that mountain, is my guess." Tighe squinted up at the thick pine woods where the fringed branches were heavy with snow. The air was crisp and clear, the silence around them complete from the shroud of snow wrapping everything in sight.

"There's something up there," Ash said, peering through her own binoculars. "But no road."

"Off-road vehicle, with no obvious sign of departing along the main road," Galen whispered. "No doubt a lookout is posted somewhere up there."

The Callahans had chosen this site for their base.

Cloistered among the trees, they felt comfortable that they couldn't be spotted. The site was also situated downwind, so their voices wouldn't carry. It was an ideal location.

But those tire tracks bothered Tighe. Something about them kept nagging at him. The tracks were fresh, and there was just one set, so the route clearly wasn't driven often. "Maybe the lookout only changes once a week. It's possible new snow covered up older tracks."

"Possible," Dante said. Tighe's twin stood next to him, lending his support. Ever since they'd decided on the mission, Dante had stuck to him like a burr, as in the old days, when it was the two of them against the world. Tighe appreciated him being there.

For his part, Dante was no longer laughing and teasing about words he'd once spoken into the wind, wishing for his brothers to be set on torturous paths to win their women. He had been much more taciturn lately. "Possible, but I'm going to postulate that something's been moved into the mountains for safekeeping," he said suddenly.

Tighe squinted up into the snow-covered forest. "Whatever it is, it's frozen now."

"Maybe some equipment," Ash said.

"Something Wolf considers a valuable target, something he wouldn't want us to have in case we attack." Falcon looked through his rifle sight, checking for movement. "He's got more backup this time. And no doubt more weapons."

Tighe looked at the sky, seeing thick clouds obscuring the stars and moon. Perfect for what they had planned.

Ash wrapped her arm through his. "It's going to be all right."

He hoped so. It was a night fit for a Shakespearean play, maybe some witches howling out of the darkness and whatever other foul luck might stand in the way. Tighe tightened his hood. He prayed he hadn't brought his family here to meet their doom.

His phone buzzed once in his pocket, signaling a text. Tighe pulled it out to peer at it.

River taken to other location. Look for small shack in the woods. F

Holy smoke. Tighe's gut clenched. He blinked, read the text again.

"You know how we planned for every contingency?" he asked.

His family's attention riveted on him. "Text from Fiona. River's been taken to a satellite location."

They all stared at him, and he read in their eyes exactly what he knew—all the careful planning had just gone up in flames. "And I don't know if this is good or bad news, but River doesn't have her backpack." He held up his phone for emphasis. "Fiona used River's cell phone. I can see several scenarios where all of the above is bad news." He took a deep breath. "Wherever River is, she doesn't have a communication device to reach us, nor weapons, either. Fiona, on the other hand, has River's backpack, and her mobile."

"That's the good news, then," Ash said. "We can communicate with *her* if we have to."

"It also means our spry and occasionally feisty aunt has a full bag of weapons, some of them incendiary. I don't think I have to spell out to any of you what the combination of Fiona and some really interesting fireworks could mean to our battle plan."

"Not to mention the side of this mountain," Jace said.

"We could be talking landslide," Ash said, her voice awed. "Like Christmas in July, complete with fireworks in the snow."

"Snowmageddon," Sloan said. "Snow, ice, tree limbs everywhere. Apocalyptic."

"Yeah," Falcon agreed. "Fiona's always liked to do things for folks to remember and talk about for years to come."

"She does like legacy-building, one-for-the-record-books stuff," Galen said, sounding very worried. "I can think of no worse combination than Fiona and a chance to take out years and years of frustration against Wolf."

"Pray she doesn't realize what she's holding in that bag," Jace said. "Her chance for revenge."

It was too terrible to contemplate. But first things first. "I'm going to follow those tracks," Tighe said. "I have a funny feeling I know what I'll find at the end of that yellow brick road."

"Wait," Galen said. "We must plan. There is no margin for error."

The family grouped together. But Tighe said, "I can't wait for a plan. Start without me." And he took off toward the mountain.

IT WAS BITTER cold in the shack, and even River's best attempts at mind control couldn't disguise the discomfort seeping into her limbs. Silence enveloped the shack after four or five hours of three men laughing raucously and, River suspected, drinking to keep off the chill. They took turns, by the sound of things, one going outside for watch detail, and the other two keeping warm. Yesterday someone had loudly plopped a tray on the rickety table just outside her room. She hadn't bothered to get up. There was no light to see by, anyway, and she wasn't going to touch whatever was on the plate.

Rhein wasn't running a very tight ship. She listened for the sounds of their activities, looking for a schedule. It seemed that every three hours the watch changed.

The only time the men paid her any attention was when she opened the door to go down the hall to the bathroom. She felt their eyes on her, watching to make certain she didn't make a dash for it. Her bedroom window was nailed shut—she'd already checked that opportunity for escape.

She was going to have to make her escape soon. Her stomach cramped and shifted, the babies uneasy in her stomach. The dull cramps had returned, and that more than anything worried River.

Something soft and delicate settled over her as she lay on the bed, like angel wings floating down on her. She sat up, peering through the darkness. It was white and shimmery, catching the tiny bit of moonlight slivering in the window. She must be dreaming, so cold she was beginning to hallucinate. River reached out to touch the magic wedding dress gratefully. "I knew you'd come," she said. "Thank you, thank you, for letting me know I'm a true Callahan."

A few twinkles sparked in the air, and she smiled, comforted.

But then the dress changed, and she realized she wasn't dreaming at all. Her black, cold-weather gear lay on the bed, the boots on the floor. She gasped and sat up.

There was only one reason her prayers had been answered. It was time to make her escape.

She went down the hall to the bathroom, making sure that her napping guard dogs woke up to take notice of her. Then she went back to her room and closed the door. She slipped the black gear on, and put the gray sweats under the ratty sheets, ruffling them so it looked as if a body was sleeping in the bed. The tennis shoes she put on the floor, as if she was snuggled up cozily. The men never came into the dark room, anyway. She smiled, pleased with the way the thick sweats bunched up the sheets. "That'll freak them out."

She listened for sounds of activity, but the shack was wrapped in a wintry silence. Her trip down the hall had revealed that Rhein was not on watch outside; he was tucked up at the small fire, a bottle of whiskey at his side. He'd looked distinctly groggy, and annoyed to be awakened by her jaunt to the washroom.

As long as Rhein wasn't on watch, she had a chance.

She waited a little while longer to give them time to be deeply into the whiskey. Then, before the sentry changed, she opened her door and crept down the hall, walking right out the back of the shack. It was dark outside, which would give her cover. She looked for the watch, figuring he'd probably be situated on the roof with binoculars. But to her surprise, he was sound asleep against a tree, sitting on an old crate of some kind, an AK-47 across his lap. River noted a flashlight lay on another crate nearby, which was used as a table. Cigarette butts were scattered about, and an empty bottle of something—probably whiskey—and a coffee mug.

There was no point in wasting good supplies. River dug down in the snow, packed a huge snowball and threw it into a tree ten feet away from the lookout. She hit the branch she'd aimed for dead-on, and ice and snow showered down. The lookout didn't even move.

She walked over, took the flashlight and melted into the woods. If she could get an hour's head start down the mountain—or maybe even more—perhaps she could make it. The sky was dark, with rolling clouds and only threads of moonlight coming through the trees. There'd be a storm by morning, and with any luck, her tracks would be obscured.

It would be as if she'd simply disappeared.

TIGHE WAS MAKING good time up the mountain. This terrain was no different than some of the other cold locations in which he'd been deployed, except that the pathway here was fairly smooth, less rocky under the thick snow.

He used no light, only night vision goggles. He didn't worry about footprints—the coming storm would take care of that.

This was the easiest assignment he'd ever had. Like any other mission, this one had a definite goal, a preferred outcome that he would achieve.

Suddenly he stopped, certain he'd heard something other than wind gusting the trees, or icy limbs falling. Whatever it was stopped, too. Or maybe he'd imagined it.

No. He didn't imagine things, and that sense of danger that had saved him many a time was screaming, a banshee curdling his ears. He stayed still, barely breathing.

The sound resumed, a steady *squish* of footfalls sinking into the snow. He leaned up against a tree, quietly pulled a Sig Sauer 9 mm from his pack and waited, tense, listening.

Shuffle…step…careful sounds of boots marching forward with determination. The strides were long when possible, the crunches lighter than a man's boots. Tighe straightened, a crazy thought dawning in his brain.

The steps were a woman's.

The only woman on the mountain who would be on a mission to get off it would be—

He took a deep breath when he heard a female voice mutter something that sounded like a prayer, a chant, a quiet invoking of spirits to keep fear at bay.

Tighe put the gun away and moved behind a tree to wait and see if a miracle was possible on this frozen night.

Chapter Seventeen

River hurried, determined to reach the bottom of the mountain, where Tighe or the other Callahans might spy her. She knew they were nearby; they had to be. The flashlight beam shone in front of her, leading the way over the snow-covered ground.

If she was wrong and the Callahans weren't here, she'd walk to the main road, try to flag down a car. It was miles away, but anything was better than being trapped in that filthy cabin with Rhein. If she could get help, maybe she could rescue Fiona.

A tall figure stepped from behind a tree, and River gasped with fear.

"River. It's Tighe."

She could hardly believe it. He reached out his arms, and she rushed into his warmth. "Tighe! How did you find me?"

"They left tire tracks. And Fiona sent us a message that you'd been moved. It wasn't hard to figure out. What are you doing here in the dark?" He hugged her close, and her knees sagged with relief.

"I got out. My guards and the lookout were asleep." She buried her face in his chest, realizing she'd held a secret fear inside her that she might not ever hold Tighe again. He kissed her, and River melted against him, relieved that he'd come to take her home. Finally, the long nightmare was over.

He broke away far too soon, but didn't let go of her hand. River craved his touch, the feel of him. "Come on. There's no time to waste, as much as I would love to hold you all night," he said.

"There'll be time enough for that when we get back to Rancho Diablo. I intend to spend plenty of time alone with you." She let him help her walk in the snow so they could make faster time. "Are you alone?"

"The whole gang is here. And Fiona's got your backpack. The others are going to get our aunt out of there, so we don't want to be late for the departure."

River put one foot in front of the other—she could only breathe, not talk. It seemed she'd been walking forever, and her stomach was cramping like mad.

"Are you all right?" Tighe asked, stopping to peer at her.

"Just a little tired." She tried to smile when he gazed into her face, pushed her hair back. "My stomach hurts a bit."

"Is it the babies?"

"I don't think so," River said, "I think it's that I haven't had a healthy meal in ages, and I've been living in dirty places." She realized she was about to cry, and wouldn't let herself. "I'm so afraid they'll discover I've left. They've got an off-road vehicle, so we have to hurry, Tighe."

She didn't want anything to happen to him, and if Rhein found out she'd left, he and his goons would come after them. He could also send word to Wolf to have the other men watch the bottom of the mountain. She wouldn't be much help to Tighe.

River tried to walk faster, telling herself that the sooner she got off the mountain, the sooner her babies and her man would be safe.

THEY GOT TO the bottom without mishap, then Tighe texted Ash that he planned to have River rest until Operation Rescue Fiona began. He was seriously worried about River. She was putting on the bravest of faces, but it didn't escape him that occasionally she stopped, rubbed her belly and took long breaths.

Anyone would be winded walking down a mountain in heavy snow, but River was in excellent condition. He remembered when he and Dante had thought the nanny bodyguards walked like panthers, strong and graceful, with long, purposeful strides. Her steps had changed, and while that was to be expected, given the circumstances, Tighe felt certain she was in pain. She wasn't the kind of woman who would complain very much when there was nothing that could be done about it, when a mission was in play.

Rage against Wolf filled him, as it always did lately, a gnawing, burning sensation that focused him on what he had to do, and also sharpened his desire to kill his uncle. He'd been forbidden to do so by his grandfather, and Tighe only hoped he would remember Running Bear's warning. The urge to end the curse that was Wolf burned strong in him.

"Sit," he told River, helping her to a fallen log well hidden from the snow-crusted path the off-road vehicle had taken up the mountain. "Someone will be here soon to help you get to the truck. Then if you need to go to a hospital, all you have to do is say the word." He knelt to look in her face. "I know this isn't the right time to tell you this, but you're beautiful, babe. The most beautiful, amazing woman I've ever known."

She smiled, her eyes glowing for just a moment. "It's a great time to hear those words. Thank you. I know it's not true—I haven't even washed my hair in three days—but you're a prince for trying to make me understand that the end is in sight."

"It's in sight, all right." He heard the sound of tires crunching through the snow behind him and turned. "Of course my sister has to spit in the eye of the tiger," he said, helping River to her feet. Ash pulled the jeep up, and he heard a door open. "Come on."

"How do you know it's Ash?"

He escorted her forward. "Because she's just a little closer to crazy than the rest of us. When I told her that I had you and was ready to go, I didn't mean for her to drive a vehicle right up where Wolf and his men could see it."

River giggled. "Ash is awesome."

"She is. And so are you."

Darkness enveloped the forest and the jeep, hopefully covering their movements. If the dirtbags on the mountain were still out like lights, then they wouldn't have notified Wolf that River had escaped and might not have a sentry posted at the front of the cabin. *Maybe, just maybe, we can get away with this.*

Ash appeared at his side, and took River's other arm to guide her over the snow. "Long time, no see," she told her. "Let's get you home."

They piled River into the jeep, and Tighe wrapped her in a blanket. Dante and Jace were posted in back, with long rifles aimed at Wolf's cabin.

Okay, so Ash hadn't completely thumbed her nose

at the devil. For the first time, Tighe began to breathe a little easier.

"Here we go," his sister said, and without turning on the lights, slowly drove toward the stakeout location. "How are you doing, River?"

"Fine. Thanks for providing the rescue party."

Tighe held River to him, keeping the blanket tight around her. She was starting to shake, from either the aftereffects of stress or the severe cold, or both. "When we reach camp, I'll get you a cup of tea."

"Sounds like heaven," River said, and laid her head against his chest.

He met his sister's gaze in the mirror. Ash appeared worried, her brows raised, then she looked back at the road.

Tighe held River, stroking her hair.

They couldn't be back at Rancho Diablo soon enough.

THIRTY MINUTES LATER, Tighe had River bundled up in the back of the truck, a cup of tea in her hand. "It's not as hot as it could be, but we're using the lighter plug instead of building a fire."

"It's perfect." She gave him a wan smile.

"I wish you'd lie down."

"I can't. I don't want to miss a thing."

Fiona's rescue would begin in a few minutes. His brothers and Ash were gearing up and checking their weapons. They'd texted Fiona one final time: Get ready. 0400.

Tighe figured they were all as ready as they could be.

"You love this, don't you?" River asked with a smile.

"I'm not going to say that my blood doesn't speed up

a little bit at the thought of getting Fiona out of there, and everybody home safe."

"You're going, right?"

"I'm sitting here with you. We'll watch the proceedings together. I'll be driving the truck when we haul ass out of here. You'll be snug as a bug in a rug in the back, waving goodbye to Wolf." At least that's how he hoped it went.

"Don't stay here because of me. I don't want you to miss anything."

He laughed. "I'll be fine. Someone needs to cover the front, and someone with decent driving skills has to get us out of here. I feel plenty useful." He patted her leg. "Besides, I'm not letting you out of my sight yet."

She smiled, and he went back to helping his brothers and sister gear up. Checked the sky, and the time on his watch. Watched the road, front and back, where they would clear out of the woods.

"Remember Grandfather's words," he reminded them. "No killing unless absolutely necessary. I feel confident we have the skills to pull this off without a single shot fired."

They nodded in understanding. Tighe studied their faces, satisfied with what he saw. "It's time," he said softly, and for one final, brief moment, they came together as a team, as a family, and stood in a circle. Tighe felt no fear; they were too strong for that.

"Here we go," he said, and his sister and brothers disappeared into the thick woods. Galen would drive the jeep, so took watch at the top of the road, his eye to his weapon as he lay on the ground, ready to fire. Tighe sat in the back of the truck, his rifle pointed toward the hideout, checking for any snipers on the roof as his family approached.

"Stay down," he told River, and she obeyed—although he noticed she didn't really lie down so much as crouch, so she could peer up over the window frame to see what was happening. Satisfied that she intended to stay put, Tighe went back to staring through the rifle sight.

He tried not to think about what he was sending his family in to do. He hoped like hell that he hadn't jinxed the mission by insisting on moving up the target date.

He refused to doubt his gut instinct, and the knowledge that had come to his spirit, that danger lay in inaction just as much as in action.

Tighe squinted, watching, waiting. Grateful for every moment of silence, because that meant his siblings might make it in and out without discovery.

And then all hell broke loose.

Chapter Eighteen

He picked up his ringing phone. "Yeah?"

"Fiona failed to mention she's had a fall," Ash said. "She's not as ambulatory as we'd thought."

He could hear the sounds of fighting in the background.

"How many operatives?"

"Two women and at least five men. I'm not saying we're pinned down, but we could use some help extracting the package."

He could hear Fiona in the background insisting that she was fine, that she could outrun all of them.

"Coming."

He handed River the rifle through the back window. "Aim for anything that comes through that door that isn't a Callahan."

She put down the window and aimed toward the hideout.

He took off through the woods, circling the open clearing in front of the cabin, his heart thundering. Loud noises seemed to shake the house; he could hear Wolf's men yelling to each other.

He didn't hear his sibling's voices, which was a good sign. When he slipped around back, the first person he came into contact with was Fiona. She was bent down behind a snow-covered barrel. "Fiona!"

"Hello, nephew!" She beamed. "I'm ready!"

She had River's backpack on her shoulders, and a grin on her face. Her rubber-soled boots were on her feet, and her hair was covered with a black hood.

"Where are you injured?" he asked her.

Her chin rose. "As I told my bossy niece, I'm fine. Don't you worry about your old aunt. I'm in better shape than all of you."

Okay. Feistiness still in place. The mission was still good. He took his aunt's arm as Ash appeared.

"Can she walk all the way to the truck?"

"Of course I can!" Fiona was indignant. "Do you think I need to be carried out of here by flying monkeys? For heaven's sake! It's a twisted ankle, that's all."

Tighe glanced at Ash. "We'll get as far as we can. See what happens."

Thick snow started falling, coming down fast, and a fierce wind sprang up.

"They're almost finished," Ash said, her finger pressed to her earpiece. "Let's move." She took Fiona's other arm.

"Just a moment," their aunt said.

"We can't wait," Ash insisted. "The team is departing and about to head out. We can't get left behind. Wolf and his men will return soon."

"That's all right. I've been here long enough. I'm in no hurry to leave just yet." She took off the backpack, rooted around inside, came up with Jace's just-in-case surprise.

Fiona looked at Ash and Tighe. "I'll be right back." She disappeared inside.

"Great Spirit," Tighe said, and it was a prayer. "If

our parents were like her, we've got some catching up to do."

"I think about that sometimes. Hurry, Aunt Fiona!" Ash yelled toward the house.

"You think she knows how to set that thing?" Tighe asked.

"I wasn't about to ask, and neither were you. Because I'm pretty sure the answer is yes."

He sighed. "It was a fairly simple device. Jace sent it along for River's use. I'm pretty sure she's baked cakes more involved than that."

Fiona reappeared with a big smile on her face. "Race you to the meet-up point."

Tighe looked at Ash over their determined aunt's head. She smiled, and they helped Fiona walk as fast as she could into the woods, Tighe covering their backs.

Once they made it deep into the woods, the snow wasn't as thick. Fiona stopped. "Just a minute."

She took out a device and pushed it.

An explosion rocked the house, and Tighe could feel the ground trembling below his feet. Fiona grinned.

"Nobody throws a party like I do," she said with satisfaction as they watched fire envelop the structure. "I'm sure Wolf will kidnap me again, because I'm the only one besides Running Bear who knows the information he wants. But I'll never be here, nor will any of the other Callahan women, ever again."

She started walking, then turned around to glance at Ash and Tighe, who were studying her handiwork. A fireball blew toward the sky when the gas stove exploded. Fiona looked pleased. "Running Bear will be so proud. Now let's go home. I can't wait to bake cookies in my own kitchen and drink my own coffee."

At the truck, Tighe handed his aunt over to Dante,

and his siblings all grabbed their seats. Tighe didn't think he'd ever been so glad to leave a place. "Everybody good?" The question was generic, but his gaze went to River in the rearview mirror.

"Yes," she said. "What caused the explosion?"

"Fiona left a party favor. When we get home, take your backpack from her, will you?"

River smiled. "Some party favor, Fiona. Good thing the snow will keep that little campfire in check."

Sitting in the front seat, Fiona looked out at her destruction as they drove away. "Wolf, you ornery son of a gun, you'll never, ever beat this family. It will happen over my cold, dead body," she murmured.

Chills shot all through Tighe. His glance met River's in the mirror, and he knew she'd felt chills, too.

AT RANCHO DIABLO the next day, Tighe felt as if he was in recovery mode, but River was just excited to be home. She ate anything he brought her, and said her stomach felt better—though he'd insisted on taking her straight to the hospital for a thorough checkup. They made an appointment in Santa Fe with a doctor who specialized in multiple births and high-risk pregnancies.

Tighe also bought the largest bottle of prenatal vitamins he could find, and several plump oranges for her to eat. "Every time I see you, I expect you to be in that rocker, with an orange and a glass of water in your hand."

River shook her head. "Will you quit worrying?"

"Absolutely not." He'd installed her in the main house, so everyone could keep an eye on her. She was next to a window, so she could sit and enjoy the warmth and the sunshine. River insisted she didn't need so much attention, that she felt like an old turtle sunning itself on a rock. The family responded by backing off a little, but making sure she was never without something to eat and drink.

River seemed thin to Tighe, but then she'd always been athletically built. He'd missed her body and he'd missed her smile like mad. It was so good to have her home.

"Fiona baked gingerbread," Tighe said.

"Oh, good." River looked expectant. "I'll get up and grab some when the timer dings."

"I'll bring you some, and a nice glass of milk."

"I'm not bed-bound yet, Tighe. Don't make me be still before it's my time."

"You've recently walked down a mountain. You've had plenty of exercise to last you for the next four months. Right now you're staying in this room with this nice fire."

"He's going to be insufferable until the babies are born," Fiona said, strolling into the room. She waved a calendar. "In view of our recent adventures, and our coming new additions," she said with a smile for River, "I am proposing moving the Christmas ball until after the babies are born."

"Don't change schedules on my behalf," River said. "I'm fine! Tighe is just being overprotective."

"It's not just that," Fiona said, "although your pregnancy is a big consideration. I'm a bit tired from all the travels, I must say. I wouldn't want to do a Christmas ball without my usual vigor." She gave them both a sly smile. "Besides, I'm thinking that a wedding might occur sooner than later? Perhaps around Christmas?"

She gave them a pointed look.

Tighe glanced at River, who slowly met his gaze.

He grinned at her. "Aunt Fiona thinks we should get married."

River didn't say anything.

"Yes," Fiona said. "Since you were wearing the magic wedding dress yesterday, which I thought looked lovely on you—"

"What magic wedding dress?" Tighe demanded. He hadn't let River out of his sight, and he hadn't seen a sign of wedding white. He wished he had.

"I'll let River tell you," Fiona said, leaving the room with a flourish of her calendar.

River gave him a slight smile. "You didn't notice?"

"Notice what?" He was truly adrift. "As much as I'd love to see you wearing any wedding dress at all, I must have been asleep. We were on the road for so long after we left Montana, I must have conked out when Ash was driving."

"Yes," River said, "and I was wearing the magic wedding dress. Do you think it's a bad sign that you didn't notice? Isn't it supposed to be obvious to my one true love that I have it on?" she teased.

"All I was thinking of was you and the babies." He frowned.

She held out her hand, and he took it. When she pulled him closer to her, he knelt beside her.

"Tighe, I agree with your aunt Fiona."

He perked up. "About a Christmas wedding?"

"Not exactly." She kissed him on the lips. "I think a wedding as soon as you can find Running Bear. I'd like to do it while I can still stand."

Tighe felt shell-shocked. "Thank you."

"Thank you?"

He pressed her palm to his lips. "Thank you for marrying me. I'll be the best husband I can be." They'd been through a lot; she'd been through more than he ever thought a fiancée of his should have to endure. "I'll make everything up to you."

"There's nothing to make up." She frowned at him. "I wish you didn't feel that there was."

He didn't know what to say. "I'll see if I can hunt up Running Bear. In the meantime, I…" He looked at her. "Did you really have the magic wedding dress on yesterday, or is Fiona pulling my leg? Because I went looking for it one day, and I couldn't find the thing. I was beginning to think it had gone AWOL and wouldn't make an appearance to work its magic for me." He blew out a breath. "I don't feel very lucky these days."

"Did you feel lucky when you rode Firefreak?"

"I felt lucky—and then I felt broken. In pieces. But I've healed. And I'm not going down that road again. Firefreak will torture other cowboys, but not this one." Tighe knelt down beside her. "You marrying me? Now that's lucky."

"Oh, Tighe." She leaned forward to kiss him. "I would support you if you decided to ride Firefreak again. I really would. I shouldn't have plotted against you." She smiled. "I had a lot of time to think about that night while I was gone, and while I shouldn't have ganged up on you, I'm glad you spent the night with me. That was a lot of fun, being seduced by a wild-eyed daredevil cowboy."

He felt his chest puff out a little. "You think I'm a wild-eyed daredevil?"

"A sexy, wild-eyed daredevil."

"Well, then." This was looking up indeed. "I think being a dad will be adventurous enough for me. I've given up Firefreak for good."

"Adventurous *and* sexy," she said, and he decided River's smile was the best part of his day.

"So you'll tell me how I missed the magic wedding dress when I return?"

She nodded. "I will. I'll be glad to spin you the yarn, though you may not believe it. Even I'm not sure I believe it. But it happened."

"I'll believe anything around here these days," Tighe said, and departed with a grin.

"The thing is," Tighe told his grandfather, when he'd located him in the canyon, "I want to marry River because I'm crazy about her. I love her. And we're having children." He straightened, realizing she'd had several tests, one of which would have probably revealed the gender of the children, which she had not shared with him. He'd have to remedy that later. "We're having triplets, and so River needs to marry me so I can be a father and a husband. It's going to be awesome."

He sat on the ledge with his grandfather, gazing out at the painted canyons and listening to the soothing sound of an eagle's cry overhead. It was peaceful here, and he had no peace inside himself. Maybe that's why he loved the canyons so much.

"What worries me is Wolf. And all the craziness, the insanity. I get a pain in my chest when I think about him taking one of my children, or one of the other Callahan kids." Tighe wasn't sure how to express his worries better than he was, but his grandfather's eyes held no judgment, no condemnation, only the patient wisdom of seeing things as they should be seen, borne of long years of experiencing life. "I hated it when Wolf was holding River."

"She's strong," Running Bear said.

"Don't I know it. Stronger than me," Tighe freely admitted. "But that's just the thing. She shouldn't have to be."

"What should River be?" Running Bear looked at him, his gaze curious.

"River should be free to be a wife and a mother. She shouldn't have to live in fear. There may never be a day when she doesn't worry about the babies as they grow up—that's normal. But I don't want her to have the extra worry of knowing Wolf is out there, waiting for us to let our guard down. It's a lot to ask of a woman."

Running Bear nodded. "It is. But River was strong before she came to Rancho Diablo."

True, but what had been asked of her since she'd been here was more than an employee should have to bear. And most certainly more than a wife should have to worry about.

"You and your brothers and sister, and your cousins, all of you deserved the chance to grow up as children with no worries," the old chief said. "We protected you, we taught you the ways. Then we prepared you for the fight. What would you say to your own children?" Running Bear's dark eyes were patient. "Would you tell them to give up? Sell the land? Give it over to the cartel?"

Tighe hadn't thought of it that way. "Is there no other option, no place in between, where they can just be children, and my wife can just be a wife?"

"Were you just a child with no cares? Or did you embrace the fight once you understood what was at stake?" His grandfather looked out across the undulating canyons that had been carved from time. "Why did you go to Afghanistan?"

"Because I believed in the mission. I believed in a

world where people could be free," Tighe said softly. "I believe everyone has a right to clean food, clean water and peace. I believe everyone on this planet has the right to raise their family, and love each other. And I fought for that."

"But the price was high."

"The price was high." Tighe nodded. "For me, it had to be paid."

"What would you tell your children? That they are above paying this price?"

"I don't want my children to be afraid. I want them to live without fear of danger."

"That is a fairy tale," Running Bear told him. "And you don't believe in fairy tales, or the supernatural life, or the ways that cannot be explained."

"I believe. Not in magic," Tighe said softly. "But I know it's important to put my faith and trust in that which I don't understand. But fairy tales for my children—is that wrong to want?"

"Even you do not believe in that," Running Bear said, "so why do you want to give them a way of life you do not know?"

"Because they might get kidnapped," Tighe confessed. "I just lost my best friend for the past three months. She's come back with a big stomach, three of my children growing inside her, and she walked down a snowy, icy mountain to save herself. Frankly, I think that's too much to ask."

"Will you not ask it of her, then?" Running Bear asked.

"I have asked it of her. I'm just not sure it's the right question to ask."

The old chief turned to face him. "Your journey is

not yet complete. It cannot be complete until you know the answers. The answers are only inside you."

They sat companionably for a while, giving Tighe a chance to chew on that bit of chief wisdom. He couldn't solve it all right now. He was too afraid for River and his unborn children. "So...I guess you heard about the parting gift Fiona left behind for Wolf?"

A slight shadow, which might have been a smile, passed over Running Bear's face. "Fiona's blood—and the blood of your parents—runs strong in your children. You must remember that. This is a family, an unbroken line, of warriors."

He rose and disappeared. Tighe stared after his grandfather for a moment, thinking about what he'd just been told.

Great. His children would follow in the family footsteps. It was a helluva combination: the past, the future and all the magic that lay between the two.

The thought of watching his children grow up, walking in the shadows of their forefathers and relatives, brought the biggest smile to Tighe's face. *Grandfather's right. I wouldn't want my children to live in a fairy tale. I want them to fight the good fight.*

It's going to be epic.

I'll hang on as hard as I can for that ride.

Chapter Nineteen

The specialist in Santa Fe ran her tests on River, and concluded the same thing she'd been told before: the babies were healthy, and so far the pregnancy was progressing normally. River smiled at Tighe as they drove back to Rancho Diablo.

"I told you there was nothing to worry about."

He grunted. "Worry is my middle name these days."

"I told you I took good care of myself in Montana."

He winced. "I don't want to think about that anymore. Can we not mention Montana?"

"That's fine by me." River looked out the window. She didn't really want to talk about the time she'd spent away from Tighe, either. But it had happened, and sometimes she felt she had feelings she needed to express to someone.

She and Fiona sat and chatted about those months often. Tighe's aunt had said they had to keep a stiff upper lip about it, that the experience would ultimately make them stronger.

"Hey, if you smile, I might tell you the gender of the babies."

He pulled over at a roadside café and her stomach

rumbled. Seemed as if she was hungry all the time now. River sighed with anticipation.

"Okay. I'm smiling," Tighe said.

"There's no smile on your face." She shook her head. "I'm waiting for the real thing."

"I smiled in Dr. Simone's office."

"When she told you we could still enjoy marital relations for at least another week."

He snapped his fingers. "That's right! I forgot!"

River laughed. "I'm pretty sure you didn't."

"Maybe not. You want some hot tea? Something to eat?" He checked his watch. "Pretty sure I need to keep you on a regular eating schedule."

She sighed. "Aren't you even curious about what the sexes of the babies are?"

"No. We're having boys." He picked up her hand, pressed a kiss to her fingertips. "Is that what you're just dying to tell me?"

"We're not having three boys."

"Three girls?" A smile spread across his face—finally.

River kissed him. "Not exactly."

He held up his hands. "I don't want to know."

"You don't?"

"I'll know in two months—at the earliest. But I'm going to do everything I can to carry you around on a cushion and get you to relax so my children stay in that nice, soft tummy of yours as long as possible." He looked at River, his smile turning sexy. "Listen, if you're not hungry, if you can wait until we get to Rancho Diablo for some of Fiona's snacks, there's no reason to eat diner food."

"What's on your mind?" River asked suspiciously.

"It just occurred to me that if we only have another week to make love, there's no time to waste."

"Then I'll wait to eat at Fiona's."

"That's my girl. Let's see if I can break some sound barriers getting home. By the way," Tighe said casually, "Running Bear said that he'd be happy to bless our union today, if you want."

River blinked. "Today?"

"Sure. There's no reason to wait, is there? Especially if the babies arrive sooner than later. February is too soon, in my opinion, because you'll only be eight months along, but the babies may be eager to see the world. I want us to be married when they decide to check out of your beautiful body."

River swallowed. "All right."

"All right?" He glanced at her. "We don't have to get married today, if you don't want to."

"Of course I want to." She looked at Tighe, feeling a bit shy. "I was just hoping to have a wedding like the other Callahan women. You know, guests, cake, magic wedding dress. All that bridal stuff. I didn't think I wanted it before, but now I feel it would be nice."

"I don't think we should wait to plan a big wedding. That could take months, and to hear Dr. Simone tell it, you won't be moving around too much for a while."

"I know. All right. Tomorrow is our wedding day." She smiled at Tighe, and he kissed her hand and drove toward Rancho Diablo.

River looked out the window and wished she could wear the magic wedding dress just one more time. When she'd put it on to escape from Wolf, she hadn't seen her dream man, her one true love. There'd been no vision, no visitation of a princely variety.

Maybe the Callahan women played up the myth.

It would be just like them to work that story for all it was worth. Of course. That's what it was, nothing more than a fairy tale.

A marriage wasn't born of fairy tales.

Then again, maybe she should try the gown on just one more time. Fiona had taken it from her when she'd gotten home, saying that the black pants and top and boots needed to have some TLC to put the magic back to rights. River wasn't certain how one put a magical dress "back to rights," but nevertheless, Fiona had seemed confident.

And River wanted to be married in the dress.

I'll ask Fiona if I can borrow it one more time. I just have to know if the magic wedding dress will turn into black fatigues again—or if I was ever meant to wear a lovely gown.

Suddenly she realized why she hadn't seen Tighe when she'd put the gown on. Tighe was nervous. He was nervous about the babies, too—he didn't want to know the sex. Didn't want to let her out of his sight—because she might get kidnapped again. Didn't want to wait to get married, because she might go into labor sooner than later.

She eyed him as he drove. *Lover, you're going to have to get a grip.*

If I have to wear black fatigues in lieu of a wedding gown, you'll have to suck it up, too.

RUNNING BEAR CAME by the next day, his face reflecting its usual inscrutability. Tighe considered his grandfather. "This is your wedding face?"

"There are men in the canyons."

"Men?" Tighe glanced at the den to make sure River

was far enough away that she couldn't hear Running Bear's warning. "Like, Wolf's men?"

"It seems so."

"I guess they have no place else to go, after Aunt Fiona's little party favor."

Running Bear nodded. "No doubt he is angry."

A lightbulb went on for Tighe. "You think Fiona may be in danger."

"I think we shouldn't overlook any possibility."

"All right." He took a deep breath. "Christmas is in three weeks. We'll send Fiona to Hell's Colony in Texas after Christmas."

"Tomorrow," Running Bear said.

Tighe had been reaching for a cup to offer his grandfather some tea, but now he hesitated. "You're really concerned."

"There is no need to trouble ourselves over this if we stay one step ahead."

"That is not going to go over well with the redoubtable aunt." He met the chief's gaze. "I'll tell her after you bless River's and my marriage today."

Running Bear nodded. "River must go, too."

Tighe blinked. "Oh, she's not going to like that."

"The risk is great."

He poured a cup of tea and put a couple of chocolate chip cookies on a plate, pushing it across the counter for his grandfather, who seated himself with an appreciative nod. "I see your point. It makes sense. But River believes she can take care of herself. She's always been strong, maybe stronger than most men. I don't think she'll go."

Running Bear nodded. "It will be hard to convince her."

Tighe went and looked out a kitchen window, staring at the snow and the icicles limning the roofs of the barns and bunkhouse. "I'll tell her after you bless us, Grandfather."

"I will take her and Fiona to Hell's Colony tomorrow. You stay here on post."

Tighe nodded. "Thank you." He wanted River and his babies to be safe. He didn't want her to leave, but at the same time, he couldn't bear the thought of her suffering another kidnapping or attack. He wanted her to relax and enjoy her pregnancy, which she hadn't been able to do yet.

He went to find River.

Two HOURS LATER, Tighe could barely believe his good fortune when River held his hand in front of their family and listened as Running Bear spoke the ceremonial words. Tears jumped into Tighe's eyes as he slipped a beautiful ring—three carats to represent their three babies—on his bride's finger.

"You're beautiful, wife."

She smiled. "You're a handsome groom, husband."

They fed each other blue cornmeal, and then it was over. Fiona rushed to hug River. "Congratulations! A new Callahan bride." She hugged her nephew. "I'm so happy for you!"

"Thank you, Aunt Fiona." He felt a tiny bit guilty. Neither River nor Fiona knew that tomorrow they'd be living in Hell's Colony in the Phillips' compound. Still, he smiled, feeling over the moon that he was finally a husband.

He and River would spend a honeymoon night together, and then she would leave. He knew it was for the best, but that didn't make it any easier.

He went to kiss his bride. "I hope you're not too disappointed that you couldn't wear the magic wedding dress. But you're still beautiful."

She glanced down at the velvety, cream-colored chemise Ash had brought from the wedding shop. He thought River was gorgeous, but he knew she'd wanted to wear the fabled gown. It couldn't be helped; Fiona said the magic wedding dress was out of commission at the moment, whatever that meant. Maybe the thing had sputtered out of magic. He didn't care—he had his sexy bride in his arms.

"I'm slightly disappointed." She smiled up at him. "But I'm a very happy wife."

"That's the way I want my woman."

"You realize you sound terrible overbearing when you call me your woman."

He smiled down at her, touching her soft, whiskey-colored hair. "I am no-holds-barred overbearing."

"What if I called you my man?"

"I wouldn't think you were overbearing at all." He kissed her again, loving that he could do this as often as he wanted. "I'm the happiest man on the planet."

She put her head on his chest, then looked up at him again. "By the way, I heard you and Running Bear talking in the kitchen."

He perked up, recognizing trouble. "Oh?"

"Yes, I did. And I just think you should know that I have no intention of leaving this house. Or you. I'll be staying right here, with my man." She giggled, and Tighe shook his head.

I knew this was exactly how that conversation was going to go.

Truthfully, he was glad, even though he knew he should press River to leave.

He'd been without her too long to give her up now.

TIGHE WASN'T GOING to say fear hadn't become a part of his life, because it was now. He stewed every second he was away from River, and she gave him grief about it when he was with her. He wanted to set a guard on her.

She refused.

He suggested having Sawyer come back to watch her, saying that Isaiah and Carlos could be folded into the huge family gathered in Hell's Colony.

She pooh-poohed that and told Tighe not to dare.

There was no one left here except for Jace, Galen, Ash and himself. Everyone had taken their families to enjoy the Christmas holidays in Texas. Burke and Fiona had packed plenty of cookies and casseroles in the freezer for them and Fiona had left plenty of instructions for River to take care of herself.

There were plenty of hands around to help out, and some foremen to ride fence, but as for keeping an eye out for trouble, Tighe couldn't say he was entirely comfortable. It never really felt like the holidays to him. He was just glad to have his wife home, reclining in the occasional puddle of sunshine that shone through the window, illuminating her and the pretty Christmas tree Fiona had put up before she left.

But his grandfather's warning was never far from his mind.

Chapter Twenty

It seemed winter would never end. The holidays had been quiet events. Now it felt as if they were hibernating, stuck in a snow globe. Tighe felt restless, caged, and he knew River surely had to feel the same. She'd kept very still—doctor's orders—since early December. Actually, ever since their wedding night, which was the last time he'd been able to make love to her.

But he wasn't complaining. The sex wasn't the issue; that would come back into their lives. What was making him crazy was the ever-present feeling that they were being watched. River was so vulnerable now, though she seemed completely relaxed. She knitted things, she read books, she wrote letters. Her favorite activity was decorating the nursery in the foreman's cabin they'd decided to renovate. It hadn't been used in years, and River thought they could easily build onto it.

Of all the bunkhouses and other outbuildings that could be renovated, the foreman's cabin was closest to the house, so Tighe had agreed. It was built in a rugged style, and on days when the snow wasn't piled thick, workers banged away, creating extra bedrooms.

And River sneakily had brought in a decorator, who was helping her create a spacious nursery for the triplets. The two of them busily studied books and paint chips and fabric selections—and every once in a while a burst of laughter would erupt, making Tighe smile.

"You can't look," River told him once when he'd walked into the den to see what all the fun was about. "You don't want to know if we're having boys or girls, so go away."

He clapped his hands over his eyes in mock horror—but not before he'd seen lots of pink and blue. And white and teal.

Then it hit him: he was actually going to be a father to three little people. He sagged onto a sofa in the upstairs library and tried to take that in.

River was almost at her due date. They had a C-section scheduled just in case, for the end of the month. Dr. Simone really didn't see River being able to carry longer than that. She said the babies were growing fast, and that they were actually quite large for triplets. Tighe puffed up with pride at the time, thinking, *Of course they'll be big, they're Callahans.* Had the doctor expected runts?

All Callahan men were big.

But he'd seen pink just a moment ago, so there were going to be girls in the picture. He saw spots just thinking about three girls. Three River types. Three fearless, hell-raising rodeo sweethearts, with River, Fiona and Ash for role models.

He broke out into a cold sweat, knowing that he would stand little chance in a home where four women ruled the roost.

"They'll wrap me around their little fingers," he muttered to himself, just as Ash walked into the room.

"What, brother dear?" she asked. "Were you talking to yourself?"

"A little. It wasn't very productive, though."

"Your beautiful bride is snoring downstairs. It's attractive."

He grinned. "I know. I love it when she does that."

"It's so soft and peaceful, isn't it?" Ash gave him a teasing glance as she fixed them both a drink. "You know, I never thought I'd see you be so happy to hit the altar."

"Wild horses couldn't have stopped me from marrying River."

"And that turquoise squash blossom necklace you got her for Christmas is gorgeous. You're really coming along." She handed him his drink and sat next to him. "Now we just need to make some little tweaks, and you really will be Prince Charming."

He shook his head. "No tweaking. I'm already Prince Charming. Tweaking at this stage ruins the prince."

"Tweaking," Ash said. "I just want you to promise me that when the babies are born, you'll quit going around with that hangdog expression on your face, like the weight of the world is on your shoulders. You're scaring River. In fact, you're scaring all of us."

"I'll try. But I'm not making any promises. I'm pretty sure my face is just my face. It does its own thing." He brightened. "River hasn't mentioned that I'm scaring her. In fact, just this morning she said I was her handsome Studly-Do-Right."

"Oh, no," Ash groaned. "I'm pretty sure she's the best wife in the world. She's propping your ego up."

He deflated again. "You think?"

"Probably. Anyway, when the babies are born, I want you to remember to smile. You'll scare the poor things."

"Of course I'll smile at the babies!" He was indignant. "They're going to love me. And think I'm the best, most handsome dad ever."

"Good. Hold on to that positive mind-set," Ash told him, "because your bride asked me if you'd take her to see the doctor."

He blinked. "We don't have an appointment today."

"I know. She said she's having twinges. Then she dozed off."

It was as if electricity zipped through him. He jumped to his feet, slammed his glass on the end table. "Why didn't you say so?"

"Because you need to smile! You're going to scare River! She needs peace and calm around her, not the beast face that's been permanently puckering your puss."

He heard his sister's words, but he was shooting down the stairs so fast he nearly took a face-plant at the bottom. Dashing into the den, he rushed to River's side, waking her. "Are you all right? What's happening?"

"Everything is fine. I called the doctor and said I was having some twinges, and she said that we should make our way over. Do you think the roads are clear enough?" River looked out the window, obviously tense.

"The roads are fine. I'll get your bag. Jace! Galen!" he bellowed, and his brothers came running. "Please help River to the jeep. Don't let her fall, or I'll hurt you." His chest was tight as he glanced around for his keys, his hat, River's bag…. Tighe looked at River. "Don't move. I'll carry you."

She shook her head. "Your sister will help me to the car, because you make me nervous and we'll both slip and go ass over applecart into the snow. Just calm down, and everything will be fine."

He hoped so.

THE BABIES WERE born that evening and Tighe thought he'd never seen such an amazing sight. Two boys and a daddy's girl, for sure. Burkett, Liam and Chloe.

He grinned at his amazing wife. "Look at these children. They're Callahans, every last ounce of them."

He was proud as he could be. It came to Tighe that he had the same rush he'd gotten when he'd been on the back of Firefreak, that same sense of sliding-down-a-slide-and-can't-turn-back-now, but this was a good sensation. It was wonderful, a wild ride, something that would be his for the rest of his life. "Thank you," he told River, kissing her. "I know you need to rest now, but I can't thank you enough for agreeing to be my wife."

She smiled. "You're a lucky man, indeed."

"Exactly what I think." Tighe took her hand in his, kissed her fingertips and remembered to do exactly what his sister had recommended: he smiled.

He smiled big as the moon.

Chapter Twenty-One

The babies changed Tighe's life in ways he'd never imagined three little tiny bundles of joy could. He brought River and the babies home after a week in the hospital, and settled them into the new house and the cozy nursery, which before now he hadn't even peeked at. He'd had no idea what magic she was cooking up, and had been too focused on her to worry about baby cribs and drapery swatches.

"Every time I go into the nursery," he told River, who was trying to do a little walking from the bedroom to the nursery to help heal her body, "I'm amazed by how much you got done. That's quite a wonderland for babies." He grinned. "You realize that had I come to view your handiwork early, I would have known exactly what we were having." She had the babies' names painted on a plaque over each white crib.

River winked at him. "I knew you wouldn't look. You had too much on your mind."

That was certainly true. To him, the births had been a far-off dream, an amorphous event he knew was coming, but like everything else, couldn't exactly plan for.

"How did you do all that?"

"I had a lot of help." She eased onto the leather sofa

she'd ordered for the den, and he sat next to her, determined to rub her legs. "For one, the Books'n'Bingo Society ladies turned me on to a great decorator. And they did all the shopping for baby gear and supplies. I can't thank your aunt's friends enough."

He grinned. "They're old hands at it."

"By the way, they've decided to put the ball off until June, the month of weddings." River situated the monitor next to her and allowed him to spread a soft blanket over her. He never let her out of his sight now. He had four people to protect, and he knew Wolf was out there somewhere; Running Bear had said so. "They're going to do a masquerade ball with some kind of scavenger hunt."

"Matters not to me. I've already been won." Tighe leaned over to kiss her, once again loving the fact that he could kiss her now whenever he wanted, for as long as he liked.

It was heaven, a great change in his life that agreed with him very much.

"Hey," he said, "I don't know if you know this, but June is the month for weddings."

River looked at him with a suspicious smile. "Didn't I just say that?"

"You know," he said, getting up next to her and wrapping his arms around her, "I think we should get married."

"We got married, Tighe. Remember?"

"Yeah. But I don't think you got married enough."

She laughed. "Enough?"

"I've waited an awfully long time to tie you down, darling. Maybe I need to double tie those knots. All the Callahan brides marry twice."

"Tighe." River sighed with pleasure as he kissed

her neck, along her collarbone, and then pretended he was going to nose around in her sweater. "I feel pretty tied. Don't you?"

"Well, we have those three little ties in there," he said, pointing to the nursery. "But I think that one day they're going to want to see video of their mom taking their father off the market."

"Really?" She raised a brow. "Not the other way around?"

He stroked her hair and smelled it, and wished he could tell her how much he loved her without sounding as if he was crazy. Which he was—for her. "Maybe the other way around."

She kissed him. "They're going to love their daddy. All kids love their daddy, but they're going to know you're awesome."

"I am, aren't I? He brightened, thought about sneaking down in her shirt a little more, figured he'd better not push his luck and settled for holding her hand instead. "I want to be able to give my kids what I never had."

River looked up at him. "Being there for them?"

He nodded. "Lately I've realized how much of a sacrifice my parents made. When I hold those babies, or I watch you holding them, I think about how terrible and wrenching it would be if we had to leave them behind."

"You're scaring me, Tighe." River curled up against his chest, and he held her tight.

"I'm not scared. I've got my own personal bodyguard. I'm feeling very safe these days." He wondered if he could make the same decision his parents had had to make. It was a high price they'd paid—all of them had paid. The alternative was to be hunted by the cartel, and worse. His parents—and the Callahan cous-

ins' parents—wouldn't have wanted that to happen to
their children. They'd chosen a life in hiding rather
than risking their family.

He saw goose pimples had risen on River's skin and
kissed them away, comforting her. "We've got Wolf on
the run. He knows what kind of women we have here
at Rancho Diablo now. You're tough, babe."

"I know. I knew what I was getting myself into when
I seduced you."

"Ah, one of my favorite words." He kissed her lips,
and then her forehead. "How long until the doctor says
I can return the favor and seduce you?"

"Easy, cowboy," River teased, and Tighe held her
close, stroking her hair as she lay on his chest. "It may
be a few months."

"We'll see if you can hold out that long," he said,
and she laughed, and then they napped together for
a whole twenty minutes until they heard sweet baby
noises on the monitor.

Tighe grinned. It was music to his ears.

THE BABIES GREW fast over the next several months, and
it seemed to River that her husband tried to capture
every minute and every action of his babies' young
lives, taking constant videos and pictures. River
thought her husband was pretty sexy, given how en-
amored he was with his children.

He barely ever left the babies—or her—alone. When
he had his post assignments, he did his job and then
hurried back home.

It had been like this for the past four months.

At first he'd said that she needed his help with the
babies while she healed. He waved off all offers of as-

sistance from the Books'n'Bingo Society ladies, and everyone else who wanted to help.

Fiona and the rest of the family had returned, and while he allowed them to help River while he was gone, he stuck close to home and insisted on being in the thick of things.

River tried to shoo him back to work, telling him that he'd had his eight weeks of maternity leave. Tighe's response was that in some countries around the world, he'd get a year.

"I'm never going to get rid of him, Fiona," she said, when his aunt came to visit and bring cookies. "I used to be a nanny bodyguard, but now I have my own personal bodyguard. He won't go anywhere unless I have four cell phones, three armed guards, two babysitters and a bat signal in a pear tree."

"It will wear off." Fiona gazed at the new babies with a smile. "He'll calm down. His twin did. Of course, Ana wasn't kidnapped for several months." The older woman looked up. "Then again, maybe he won't get over it anytime soon."

"It could get worse over time." The thought bloomed, large and worrisome. "Can you imagine how he'll be when Chloe wants to date?"

"Well, she just won't," Fiona said, laughing. "At least not without her father in the backseat."

They giggled together. River smiled at Tighe's aunt. "Did I ever tell you how much I appreciated you keeping my spirits up in Montana?"

"The spirit is important. That's what Running Bear always says." Fiona sat down with a cup of tea and rocked in one of the new white rockers, complete with ruffled teal cushions. "Speaking of spirits, did you know Storm Cash offered to sell us the land across the canyons? He was dead set on getting that parcel, all twenty thousand acres, and now he's told me he'd like to sell. He's giving us first right of refusal. But he didn't have the land long enough to make a profit or clear his commission. I'm not sure what's up with that old goat."

River shook her head. "Tighe has never mentioned it, so I don't think he has any better idea."

Fiona sipped her tea. "I'm suspicious that Storm planted his niece over here, too. I'm not certain, but I believe Sawyer's got a target drawn on Jace."

"I'm not sure how I can help, Fiona. I don't know anything about all that."

"Here's the thing," she said, setting down her cup and reaching for Burkett when he started up a tiny squall. "I feel a cold chill coming from that side of the property."

"You mean from Storm?"

Fiona nodded. "Yes."

"Talk to Tighe. Maybe he can find something out."

"I was wondering if you'd talk to Sawyer."

River hesitated. "Me? And ask what?"

"Just see where her interests lie. What's on her mind. She just might let something slip."

"I can talk to her," River said. "But Kendall might know more, since she's Sawyer's employer."

Fiona made faces at Burkett to get him to smile, which he was too young to do. "You know that you and Tighe would be up for ownership of those twenty thousand acres, if Rancho Diablo takes them on. You'd have your own real house."

River blinked. "That would be up to Tighe, Fiona. I have a feeling he won't want to be farther from the main house than necessary." She could pretty well bank on Tighe not wanting her and the children to be across the canyons.

"Imagine having your own place, though. Your very own. Not part of a conglomerate, where everybody has a piece of everything. Stake your own claim, as it were."

"Fiona, are you asking me to spy on Sawyer in lieu of a favorable outcome to the ranch raffle you've been trying to set up for the Chacon Callahans all along?"

"Yes, I am," Fiona said. "Just something to consider." ·

River took that in. "I don't see how this helps Jace."

"It helps all of us to know whether the Cashs are friend or foe," Fiona said. "It's important to know who's on your side."

River closed her eyes, then opened them. "Fiona, I spent many months with you in Montana. We spent a lot of time talking to each other, and I believe I've gotten to know how you think. You want to keep Sawyer and Jace apart."

"Well," the older woman said slowly, "now that you mention it, yes. I don't want my nephew falling for a woman who is out to get to us through him."

"Isn't that Jace's business? Who he falls for?"

"Jace is a smart man, but he's not going to be able to withstand the amount of feminine firepower Sawyer's aiming at him. I saw her the other day taking a basket lunch out to him in the barn." Fiona looked outraged. "Every woman knows the fastest way to a man's heart is through his stomach, and my nephews are all very susceptible to that type of lure."

"I never cooked for Tighe."

"That's right. You caught my nephew fair and

square, without lures." Fiona nodded. "Believe me, I recognize a trap being carefully set when I see it."

River laughed. "Fiona, you're a treat. Don't ask me to help you with keeping Jace and Sawyer apart. I can't do that, not even for a house of my own on a few acres of land, tempting though it is. Ask Ashlyn. She's always up for a plot."

Fiona sighed. "I think you should accept the challenge. You're a new Callahan, and a new mother. No one will suspect you."

"I'm so sorry, but no." River shook her head with a huge smile. "I don't even know if Tighe wants any of that land over there. But even if he did, he'd want to win the raffle fair and square."

"Honorable of him," Fiona grumbled. "What if Sawyer's up to no good? And she snags Jace?"

"Then you'll welcome her to the family, just as you have welcomed me." River patted her hand.

Fiona sniffed. "Yes, we have. I guess we could welcome Sawyer. Although perhaps not."

"Anyway, I've given up subterfuge. Didn't you know?" River smiled. "I gave up on plotting over Callahans when I tried to keep Tighe off his dream bull. You see how that turned out for me. He still rode that animal, nearly got himself squashed, and now I'm married to him."

The two of them shared a laugh. "And in that regard, what's this I hear about another wedding?" Fiona asked.

River smiled. "Tighe wants to do it again. He thinks we need our marriage vows on video, and pictures of it for the children when they grow up."

"A fine idea, indeed," Fiona said. Her expression

turned cagey. "I imagine you'll want to borrow the family fairy-tale frock?"

"I've already borrowed it once," River said with a fond smile. "Although it was all-weather gear and black, I certainly appreciated the chance to wear it."

"Clearly, it's meant to be," Fiona said, "or the gown wouldn't have transformed itself for you. If anything, I believe you should try it on sooner than later, my girl. There's no time to waste."

"No time to waste?" River blinked. "Certainly there's no rush. We're already married, so it's not like I need the fairy dust and the vision of my one true prince, right?"

Fiona sucked in a breath. "Oh, my dear, there can never be enough magic in one's life. You just remember I told you that. Magic is the stuff of dreams. It's the air we breathe, and the hope that keeps our hearts beating. Now," she said, her expression hopeful, "can I help you plan this wedding?"

River smiled. "I can't imagine anyone else I'd rather have helping me plan the perfect wedding." She hugged the woman she'd come to know so well over the long months in Montana. "Thank you, Fiona, for everything."

"Thank *you*," she replied crisply, "for wrangling my nephew to the altar, and for bringing these three adorable Callahans to our family."

Tighe strode in, a little sunburned from working outside, a bit rumpled in his nicely fitting blue jeans, straw Resistol and blue work shirt. He was the sexiest man River had ever seen, and when he mouthed *I love you* to her over Fiona's head as he hugged his aunt, River felt like the luckiest woman in the world.

She smiled at Fiona, then at her babies. From plot to stop Tighe from riding, to happily married wife, her life as a Callahan was magical indeed.

Epilogue

The day of their wedding—second wedding—River hadn't yet tried the magic wedding gown on again. Fiona had told her to but there was no need. Hadn't she already worn it?

It would be perfect.

Any bride would be anxious not trying on her wedding dress until the big day, but River trusted the gown.

Now was her moment. Outside, white tables basked in sunshine for guests, who'd arrived on this beautiful balmy day to celebrate another Callahan wedding. The cousins had arrived from Hell's Colony, and Rancho Diablo literally crawled, hopped, jumped and squealed with children.

River's babies were being passed around by delighted guests eager to get their hands on them. There were lovely cakes and enough food to feed all of Diablo.

It was a perfect day—if the dress worked out.

She had the pictures she'd taken on her cell phone in Montana to dream by. So now she was in the attic, ready to step into the magical Callahan world of enchantment.

She pulled the zipper on the bag down, and gasped when she saw twinkles inside. Soft music played somewhere, enticing her to lift the gown out. She did, gasping with joy when she realized the dress looked exactly as it did in the photos—and the way it looked in her most fervent dreams. Elegant, white, long, gorgeous, the gown beckoned her to step into it.

River did, easing the garment slowly up her body, breathing in the fairy tale. No black fatigues this—this dress was meant to be worn by her, casting her in softness and beauty. Even her dreams of this had never been so beautiful.

She went to the cheval mirror, her eyes widening at the splendor reflected there. It seemed that light and sparkles bounced off the fabric, scattering twinkles of magic across the floor.

Tighe walked into the attic, and she whirled to face him. "I'm so glad you're here!"

He smiled, her handsome, wild-man husband, who would forever be hers. "If I never told you that I love you," River said, "I do love you, Tighe. When you came to rescue me, I knew you were a prince among men, but I fell in love with you when you were tossed off that stupid bull. Actually, I've been in love with you for a very long time."

She drank him in with hungry eyes, her tall, handsome husband who looked fiercely sexy in his tux. But she thought he was sexy all the time—and never so much as when he was holding their babies.

"I just wanted you to know," River said. "I couldn't wait another moment to tell you." She went to kiss him, show him that he was the man of her dreams—but then he was gone.

River smiled. She'd had her vision of her dream man. She was finally a real Callahan bride—and she would be, forever.

Tighe loved it when River said *I do* at the altar. It was a moment that would forever be burned into his memory. He'd waited so long to win her—and when she said her vows in front of all their friends and family and their three tiny babies, he laughed out loud from joy.

He'd hired two videographers to capture that moment from every angle. He didn't want to miss a single word of her becoming his.

"I have a gift for you," River told him as they walked toward the canyons so they could be alone for a moment.

"I know you do," Tighe said, "and believe me, I can't wait to collect on our honeymoon."

She laughed and shook her head. "No, I really have a gift for you. I hope you like it."

He let her lead him to the getaway truck they'd parked near the bunkhouse, hoping his brothers and sister wouldn't find it. They had, decorating it with streamers and Just Married signs. "They found our getaway vehicle, after all."

"We didn't really think we'd get away with a clean ride for our honeymoon."

"No." He studied his beautiful bride. "So that's the magic wedding dress."

"Yes, it is." River smiled at him, her gaze full of sexy secrets.

"So...is it true?"

"Is what true?" River asked, and he knew she was tormenting him.

"Is the legend true? Did you see your one true love?"

She laughed. "Not telling."

"It doesn't matter," he said, drawing her into his arms for a sweet kiss. "I always knew I was your one

true love, even if it took you a really long time to figure it out."

"Oh, I knew," River said. "I just wanted you to finish your journey thing."

"I have. I found what I was looking for." He kissed
her, wanting to hold her forever. "I love you so much.
Have I told you?"

"Yes," River said, laughing. She pulled away from
him. "Let me give you your gift."

"You're supposed to stay in my arms and give me
a gift," he groused, but he let her go. She reached into
the back of the truck and pulled a large, brown-paper-
wrapped frame from the truck bed. "What's this?"

"The gift. Open it and see."

He unwrapped the paper, and grinned.

It was a very large black-and-white photo of him on
Firefreak, at the very moment the bull had burst from
the chute. Tighe's hat was on, his arm was up, and Firefreak was in full kick.

"The beginning of my journey." Tighe smiled. "I
can't believe you took this. Thank you for capturing
my moment of glory."

"Believe me, I had to act fast. I only had three
seconds," River said with a smile, "but it was quick
enough to catch you."

"Don't I know it," Tighe said. "Don't I know it. And
I do love being caught."

He put the picture back in the truck and pulled his
wife close. In the distance he saw a shimmering of
color, a scattering of stardust or something that looked
suspiciously like fairy dust on the wind. He heard the
black Diablos thundering in the canyons, and then he
saw Running Bear and his parents, smiling at him in
congratulations.

They waved and disappeared, but the sound of hooves thundered on as he held River, etching the memory of what he'd seen into his soul. It was magic, and he believed again, every word and every way that he'd always known in his heart.

"Let's go back and find our children, gorgeous," he said, and they walked back home, eager to hold the next generation of Callahans close.

It was just the way he'd always known magic should be.

Enchanting.

* * * * *

Watch for the next story in
Tina Leonard's CALLAHAN COWBOYS *miniseries,*
A CALLAHAN CHRISTMAS MIRACLE,
coming November 2013, only from
Harlequin American Romance!

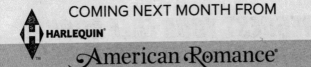

COMING NEXT MONTH FROM

HARLEQUIN

American Romance®

Available October 1, 2013

#1469 TWINS UNDER THE CHRISTMAS TREE
The Cash Brothers • by Marin Thomas
Conway Cash is ready to settle down with a good woman, but he's dead set against being a dad. So why does his blood boil when his single-mom pal Isi Lopez starts dating someone else?

#1470 BIG SKY CHRISTMAS
Coffee Creek, Montana • by C.J. Carmichael
Jackson Stone shouldn't be attracted to Winnie Hayes. After all, he was responsible for her fiancé's death. But he has a chance at redemption—and to be the man Winnie and her son need.

#1471 HER WYOMING HERO
Daddy Dude Ranch • by Rebecca Winters
Kathryn Wentworth will do anything to protect her son. Can she count on help from Ross Livingston to escape her old life and start a new one—with him?

#1472 A RANCHER'S CHRISTMAS
Saddlers Prairie • by Ann Roth
Gina Arnett wants to sell the ranch she recently inherited, but she's unprepared for the persuasive ways of ranch manager Zach Horton, who made a promise to do everything in his power to convince her to keep it.

HARCNM0913

REQUEST YOUR FREE BOOKS!
2 FREE NOVELS PLUS 2 FREE GIFTS!

HARLEQUIN

American ★ Romance®

LOVE, HOME & HAPPINESS

YES! Please send me 2 FREE Harlequin® American Romance® novels and my 2 FREE gifts (gifts are worth about $10). After receiving them, if I don't wish to receive any more books, I can return the shipping statement marked "cancel." If I don't cancel, I will receive 4 brand-new novels every month and be billed just $4.74 per book in the U.S. or $5.24 per book in Canada. That's a savings of at least 14% off the cover price! It's quite a bargain! Shipping and handling is just 50¢ per book in the U.S. and 75¢ per book in Canada.* I understand that accepting the 2 free books and gifts places me under no obligation to buy anything. I can always return a shipment and cancel at any time. Even if I never buy another book, the two free books and gifts are mine to keep forever.

154/354 HDN F4YN

Name _____ (PLEASE PRINT)

Address _____ Apt. #

City _____ State/Prov. _____ Zip/Postal Code

Signature (if under 18, a parent or guardian must sign) _____

Mail to the **Harlequin® Reader Service:**
IN U.S.A.: P.O. Box 1867, Buffalo, NY 14240-1867
IN CANADA: P.O. Box 609, Fort Erie, Ontario L2A 5X3

Want to try two free books from another line?
Call 1-800-873-8635 or visit www.ReaderService.com.

* Terms and prices subject to change without notice. Prices do not include applicable taxes. Sales tax applicable in N.Y. Canadian residents will be charged applicable taxes. Offer not valid in Quebec. This offer is limited to one order per household. Not valid for current subscribers to Harlequin American Romance books. All orders subject to credit approval. Credit or debit balances in a customer's account(s) may be offset by any other outstanding balance owed by or to the customer. Please allow 4 to 6 weeks for delivery. Offer available while quantities last.

Your Privacy—The Harlequin® Reader Service is committed to protecting your privacy. Our Privacy Policy is available online at www.ReaderService.com or upon request from the Harlequin Reader Service.

We make a portion of our mailing list available to reputable third parties that offer products we believe may interest you. If you prefer that we not exchange your name with third parties, or if you wish to clarify or modify your communication preferences, please visit us at www.ReaderService.com/consumerschoice or write to us at Harlequin Reader Service Preference Service, P.O. Box 9062, Buffalo, NY 14269. Include your complete name and address.

HAR13R

A sixth sense told Conway he was being watched. He opened his eyes beneath the cowboy hat covering his face. Two pairs of small athletic shoes stood side by side next to the sofa.

"Is he dead?"

"Poke him and see," whispered a second voice.

Conway shifted on the couch and groaned.

"He's alive."

"Maybe he's sick."

"Look under his hat."

"You look."

Conway's chest shook with laughter. Small fingers lifted the brim of his hat and suddenly Conway's gaze clashed with the boys'. They shrieked and jumped back.

He pointed to one kid. "What's your name?"

"Javier."

Conway moved his finger to the other boy.

"I'm Miguel. Who are you?"

"Conway Cash."

Javier whispered in his brother's ear, then Miguel asked, "Why are you sleeping on our couch?"

"Your mom wasn't feeling well, so I stayed the night."

"Javi…Mig…. Where are you guys?" Isi's sluggish voice rang out a moment before she appeared in the hallway.

"Mom, Conway Cash slept on our couch."

"It was nice of Mr. Conway to stay, but I'm fine now." Isi sent him a time-to-leave look.

Conway stood and handed her a piece of paper. "Your sitter left this for you last night. She wanted you to read it first thing in the morning."

While Isi read the note, Conway said, "I'd really like to make it up to you for what happened last night. Is there anything I can—"

Isi glanced up from the note, a stunned expression on her face.

"What's wrong?" he asked.

"Nicole quit. She's moving to Tucson to live with her father."

"Maybe your mother could help out with the boys."

"I told you a long time ago that I don't have any family. It's just me and the boys." She paused. "You offered to help. Would you watch the boys until I find a replacement sitter?"

Babysit? Him? "I don't think that's a good idea."

"It would be for two or three days at the most."

"I don't know anything about kids."

"Never mind." Her shoulders sagged.

Oh, hell. How hard could it be to watch a couple of four-year-olds? "Okay, I'll watch them."

She flashed him a bright smile. "You'll need to be here by noon on Monday."

"See you then." Right now, Conway couldn't escape fast enough.

Find out if Conway survives his new babysitting duties in
TWINS UNDER THE CHRISTMAS TREE
by Marin Thomas
Available October 1, 2013, only from
Harlequin® American Romance®.

American Romance®

A Holiday for Healing and New Beginnings

Jackson Stone will always be grateful to the Lamberts, who took him in when he was just a kid. But since the accident that killed his foster brother, Brock, he stays away from the family at Coffee Creek Ranch. Especially now that Brock's former fiancée, Winnie Hays, is back in town with her little boy. The simmering attraction between them may surprise Winnie, but Jackson fell for her at first sight years ago. Can this Christmas be a time of healing and a new beginning for both of them?

Big Sky Christmas

by C.J. CARMICHAEL

Available October 1, 2013, only from Harlequin® American Romance®.

HARLEQUIN®

American Romance®

A rancher comes to her rescue.

At the magnificent Wyoming dude ranch run by
Ross Livingston and two fellow ex-marines, families
of fallen soldiers find hope and healing. When lovely
widow Kit Wentworth and her son arrive, Ross
immediately finds himself drawn to them. Soon he's
able to bring young Andy out of his shell—and touch
Kit's heart as no other man has.

Her Wyoming Hero
by REBECCA WINTERS

Available October 1, 2013, only from
Harlequin® American Romance®.

HAR75475